'It's a surreal and strange tale that works because its author, Carnegie and Costa children's Book Award shortlisted Lissa Evans, is a **comic genius.** This book is seriously laugh out loud funny and the writing **sparkles** with wit. A surprising, hilarious read to be savoured.' *Book Trust*

'It's eccentric, **fast-paced** and full of big set pieces as well as some lovely, quieter moments of tenderness and bravery. It's a **celebration** of kindness, family, and being true to yourself; all while being very, very funny.' *Scoop*

'*Wed Wabbit* has all the makings of a **modern classic** and deserves to be well rewarded on **prize** shortlists.' Editor's Choice, Book of the Month in *The Bookseller* magazine

## ALSO BY LISSA EVANS

# WED WABBIT

www.**davidficklingbooks**.com

*To Martha and Nell and Stephen,*
*who read* Wed Wabbit *first.*

Wed Wabbit
is a
DAVID FICKLING BOOK

First published in Great Britain in 2017 by
David Fickling Books,
31 Beaumont Street,
Oxford, OX1 2NP

www.davidficklingbooks.com

Hardback edition published 2017
This edition published 2018

Text © Lissa Evans, 2017
Cover illustration © Sarah McIntyre, 2017
Map illustration © Tomislav Tomic, 2017

978-1-910989-44-9

1 3 5 7 9 10 8 6 4 2

Papers used by David Fickling Books are from well-managed
forests and other responsible sources.

DAVID FICKLING BOOKS Reg. No. 8340307

A CIP catalogue record for this book is available from the British Library.

Printed and bound in Great Britain by Clays, Ltd, St Ives plc.

# WED WABBIT

## LISSA EVANS

d|b
FICKLING

David Fickling Books

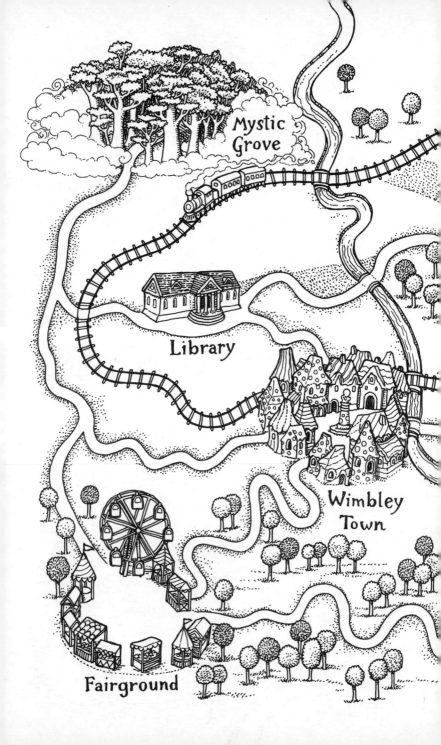

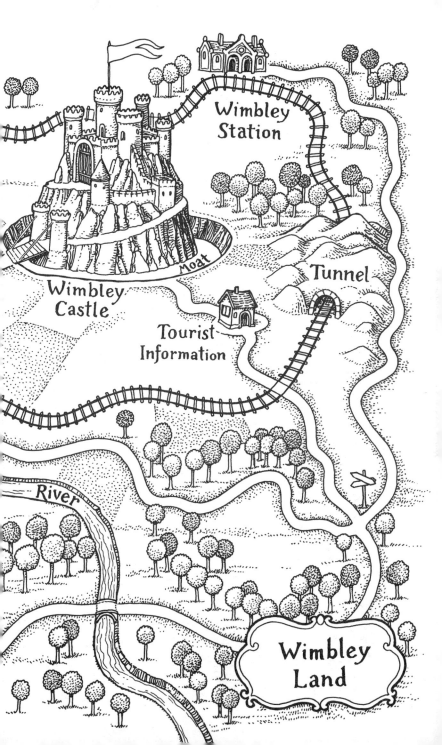

Wimbley Station

Wimbley Castle

Moat

Tunnel

Tourist Information

River

Wimbley Land

# ONE

It was such an ordinary evening, but every detail of it would matter; every detail would become *vital*.

'Wimbley Woos,' Minnie was wailing from her side of the bedroom. 'Wead me Wimbley Woos!'

'In a minute,' said Fidge. 'You're supposed to be drinking your milk.'

'But it's all warm and it's got a skin on top and it's *wevolting*.'

'All right, I won't be long.'

Fidge was packing. In just under thirty-six hours, her mother, her sister (aged four) and herself (aged ten and a half) were due to go on what was likely to be their best holiday for years and she wanted to be ready. She also wanted to try out a high-density packing technique she'd seen on a programme about mountaineers. What you did was roll up each item of clothing into an incredibly tight sausage, secured with an elastic band; you then fitted the sausages in next to each other, like a bundle of sticks. Fidge was going to attempt to put her entire holiday wardrobe into the very small backpack she used for school lunches. This was partly because she liked a challenge, and partly because she knew that her mother's luggage would (as usual) consist of a huge assortment of random bags, while Minnie never went anywhere without an armful of toys, which she then dropped at five-second intervals. *Somebody* had to have both arms free for emergencies.

'Wead me Wimbley Woos. Pleeeeeeease.'

'Not Wimbley Woos *again*. Ask Mum.'

'Sorry, Fidge, I can't,' called her mother from the living room, 'I've got to finish making this hat by tomorrow morning, it's for a bride's mother and she's terribly fussy.'

Fidge groaned and got to her feet.

Her sister's side of the room was spectacularly untidy. As Fidge picked her way across to the bed there was a loud squeak.

'Don't twead on Eleanor!' screamed Minnie.

'Well, don't leave her lying on the floor,' said Fidge, irritably. She stooped to pick up Eleanor, who was a purple elephant with a pink skirt, huge long pink eyelashes and a pink fluffy hair-do.

'She's asleep,' said Minnie. 'Wed Wabbit made them all go to bed early because they'd been naughty.'

'Oh.' Fidge looked down and realized that the teddies and dolls had been arranged in long rows, as if in a dormitory. Even the dolls' buggy was lying on its side, covered with a blanket; next to it, a silver bus with pink wheels had a little pillow under its front bumper. As usual, only Wed Wabbit was in bed with Minnie.

'OK,' sighed Fidge, sitting on the bed and plopping the elephant down beside her. 'You sure you want this book? We must have read it eight million times.'

'I want it.'

'How about I just read two pages?'

'No.'

'Five pages?'

'Mum! Fidge is being mean!'

'*Please* Fidge, just read her the whole book, it's not that long,' called their mother, sounding weary.

Fidge pulled a face, opened *The Land of Wimbley Woos* and started to read the horribly familiar lines.

*'In Wimbley Land live Wimbley Woos*
*Who come in many different hues*
*In Yellow, Pink and Green and Blue*
*In Orange, Grey and Purple too.'*

The first picture showed a group of happy-looking Wimblies. Each was a different colour, but they were all shaped like dustbins with large round eyes and short arms and legs, and

3

they radiated a sort of idiotic jollity. Fidge turned the page and continued reading in a bored, rapid mutter.

*'Yellow are timid, Blue are strong*
*Grey are wise and rarely wrong*
*Green are daring, Pink give cuddles*
*Orange are silly and get in muddles.*
*Purple Wimblies understand*
*The past and future of our land.'*

'Wead it pwoply, with *expwession,*' commanded Minnie, who could almost certainly pronounce the letter 'r' if she really tried, but who was too used to people going 'ohhhhhhh, how cuuuuuuuute' whenever she spoke, to want to make the effort.

Fidge carried on reading, with a fraction more feeling.

*'Many talents make a team*
*So Wimbley Woos can build their dream*
*By sharing skills, plans, gifts and arts*
*And caring for each other's* farts.*'*

'It's not "farts"!' shouted Minnie, outraged. 'It's *"caring for each other's* HEARTS".'

'If you know it that well then you don't need me to read it to you, do you?'

'But Wed Wabbit wants to hear it too.'

'Does he?' Fidge looked at Wed Wabbit, who was sitting

next to Minnie. He was very large and made of maroon velvet, with huge stiff ears, long, drooping arms and legs and tiny black eyes. He was her sister's favourite toy, bought from a charity shop two and a half years ago, just a week after their father died. Minnie had spotted the rabbit in the shop window and had darted in and wrapped her arms round him and hadn't let go. He'd been her favourite toy ever since, but perhaps because the awfulness of that week still sat like a weight on Fidge's head, she'd never liked Wed Wabbit. Most soft toys (in Fidge's experience) looked either smiley or sad, but Wed Wabbit had a horribly smug expression, like a clever child who knows he's the teacher's favourite and never, ever gets told off. She avoided his gaze and turned the page to an illustration of a group of Wimbley Woos scratching their heads.

'Oh, here's the bit where they try to think of a birthday present for the King of the Wimblies,' she said, with fake excitement. 'I wonder what they'll come up with? Dinner for two at a top sushi restaurant? A personalized number plate?'

'Wead it to me.'

'A spa weekend?'

'Please,' said Minnie, placing a small hand on Fidge's arm. '*Please* wead my book.'

And because Minnie (when she wasn't showing off, or being annoying or screechy or whiny) was really quite sweet, Fidge stopped mucking around and read the whole of it.

For the eight millionth time.

Over the course of twenty irritating pages the Wimbley

Woos organized a huge game of hide and seek as their surprise gift for the King, had a big celebration picnic, and sang their deeply soppy Wimbley Woo song as the sun set behind the lollipop-shaped trees of Wimbley Land.

*'Wimbley Woo! Wimbley Woo!*
*Pink and Green and Grey and Blue*
*Yellow and Orange and Purple too*
*A rainbow of sharing in all we do!'*

Fidge turned the page and looked at the last picture. It showed a mixed crowd of Wimblies standing on a hill looking up at the moon. At some point, Minnie had drawn a moustache on all the purple ones.

Minnie herself was almost asleep. Fidge tucked her in, slid the book onto the cluttered bedside table and then snatched it up again; amongst the junk was a small carton of juice and it was now on its side, and a pool of orange was spreading over the table top. Hastily, Fidge picked up the carton and then looked around for something to blot the juice with. Wed Wabbit seemed to catch her eye, his smirk as infuriating as ever, and before she knew what she was doing, she'd grabbed him by the ears and was pressing him down onto the spill. The effect was miraculous: Wed Wabbit acted like a huge sponge. The pool shrank steadily and then disappeared without trace, the orange making no stain at all on the dark-red velvet. Fidge, feeling relieved but a bit guilty, checked that

6

Minnie was definitely asleep, and then sat Wed Wabbit on the radiator and went back to her packing.

They were going on an outdoor activities holiday. Her mother and Minnie were going to potter round and play in the children's pool and Fidge was going to learn how to canoe, dive, abseil, climb, navigate, pot-hole and go-cart. She took an old T-shirt from the drawer and began to roll it very, very tightly. She had to leave enough space for the flippers her mother had promised to buy her.

It wasn't until the next afternoon that the terrible thing happened.

# TWO

Fidge looked like her dad. In old photographs, you could see the family divide: Mum and Minnie were both fair and curly-haired and round-faced, while Fidge and her dad were dark and straight-haired and angular. 'Two balls of wool and two lengths of string' was how he'd always described the four of them. He'd been funny and practical, the sort of person who always planned ahead, checked maps, wrote lists, tested equipment, kept spares, mended punctures, oiled hinges and read instructions. 'String holds things together and keeps them neat and organized,' he'd said. When Mum had wanted to name her daughters after figures from Greek and Roman mythology, he'd agreed, as long as he could give them short, sensible nicknames.

So 'Iphigenia' had become 'Fidge' and 'Minerva' had become 'Minnie'.

He'd been a fireman, and as strong as a carthorse before he got ill.

Minnie couldn't really remember him, though she pretended she could; Fidge had been eight when he died, and she remembered him all the time. And as the only piece of string left in the family, she tried to keep things neat and organized.

Which was why going shopping with her mother and Minnie was always so massively irritating.

'Ooh now,' said Mum, passing a fruit stall and then doubling back, 'wouldn't it be nice to have some strawberries for tea? They're selling off the last punnets cheap.'

'But we've still got to get Minnie's sandals,' said Fidge, 'and then my flippers, and you haven't even finished packing yet and we're going on holiday *tomorrow*.'

'Stwawbewwies!' shouted Minnie.

'Honestly, we'll only be five minutes,' said her mother, joining the queue.

Fidge rolled her eyes and looked at her list again:

> Bread for sandwiches ✓
> Nit comb (just in case) ✓
> Sandals
> Flippers

Only four items all together, but with Mum and Minnie's

usual lack of urgency, they'd bought at least nine other things and had taken all afternoon about it; both Mum and Fidge were laden with bags. Minnie wasn't carrying any shopping, but that's because she was already carrying Eleanor Elephant, Wed Wabbit and a toy mobile phone encrusted with plastic diamonds and twinkling with pink lights. When you pressed a button on the side of it – which Minnie did at least once a minute – it went:

### NING **NANG** NINGETY **NANG** NINGETY NINGETY **NANG**

After the strawberries came the shoe shop, in which Minnie was so happy about her new sandals that she did a dance which made all the other customers say 'aaaah', and then they set off for the shop that stocked flippers. They were nearly there when Minnie screamed.

'Look!' she gasped, pointing at a bookshop window, and then galloping over to it and squashing her face against the glass. 'Wimbley Woooooooos.'

The whole window was filled with tiny plastic Wimblies on a fake grass landscape. A toy train dawdled on a circuit around them, a grey Wimbley waving from the back of it. At the centre of the display was propped a brand-new pop-up edition of *The Land of Wimbley Woos*.

'Oh,' said Minnie, in ecstasy, dropping Eleanor Elephant. Fidge picked it up, just as Minnie dropped her plastic phone. 'It's so lovely . . .' sighed Minnie.

They had to go in and buy the book, of course. And then Minnie refused to leave the shop window until the train had been round another ten times. So by the time they got to the flippers place, it was closed.

'Oh, Fidge,' said Mum, looking stricken. 'I'm so sorry, love, everything took longer than it ought to have done. I always do this, don't I?'

Fidge stood hunched, arms folded, trying to look unbothered. She'd found, over the past couple of years, that if she looked unbothered, then she generally felt unbothered, and if she *felt* unbothered then it didn't leave room for feeling other, more horrible things.

'Doesn't matter,' she muttered.

'I'm sure they'll sell them at the holiday centre.'

'OK.'

Her mother tried to give her a hug and then straightened up and smiled rather sadly. 'It's like cuddling a cardboard box,' she said. 'You're all corners.'

They set off again, Minnie chattering, trying to look at her new book as she walked, and Fidge lagging behind, not saying much. When Minnie dropped Wed Wabbit, and didn't notice, Fidge found herself giving him a bit of a kick along the pavement. He spun round and lay looking up at her, with his usual smug expression. And instead of stooping to pick him up, she booted him a second time. She'd only meant to give him a bit of a prod but it turned out to be the sort of kick that you could never do deliberately, however hard you tried – the sort of kick that might have been produced by a professional footballer. Wed Wabbit shot in a perfectly straight line along the pavement, between Mum and Minnie, over the kerb and halfway across a zebra crossing.

And Minnie ran after him.

# THREE

The noise.

The noise was horrible.

A scream from Mum and a shriek of brakes, an ugly thud, the crunch of glass, a shocked chorus of yells from passers-by.

The silence was worse – the fact that Minnie didn't scream at all, but lay where she'd been flung, one leg oddly-angled, and around her an arc of scattered toys.

After that, there were running footsteps, panicked shouts and the yelp of a siren – people, people everywhere and in the midst of them, Fidge standing as if carved from concrete, still clutching the shopping bags, the plastic handles carving deep red grooves into her fingers.

'Fidge!' shouted her mother, appearing suddenly out of

the crowd and grabbing her arm. 'Into the ambulance with us, come *on*, love,' and Fidge stumbled forward, tripping on the ambulance steps. The paramedic helped her up, and sat her on a little tip-up seat opposite where Minnie lay on a stretcher, dried blood crisping her curls, a clear plastic mask over her face.

'It was my fault,' said Fidge.

Her mother didn't seem to hear, and in any case, at that moment Minnie jerked her head and started crying and Mum went red and started crying too, and the paramedic said, 'You might not think it now, but that's a *really* good sound to hear.'

At the hospital, Minnie was wheeled off behind a curtain with Mum, and Fidge sat with the bags of shopping. Her head seemed to be full of fog, her thoughts stumbling around in hopeless circles.

Hours went by. Sunset filled the waiting room with orange light. Her mother appeared briefly, tried to smile (she *always* tried to smile), said that Minnie hadn't really woken up yet, and then disappeared again. The sky outside turned a pale lavender, then dark purple, then black. The only noise in the room was the whine of the vending machine.

'Fidge?' It was a man's voice. Stiffly, as if her neck had rusted up, she looked round, and her heart would have sunk, except that it couldn't get any lower than it was already.

Uncle Simon was standing in the doorway of the waiting room, holding an orange plastic bag, a small bottle of antiseptic spray and a box of tissues. He blinked anxiously and took half a step towards Fidge, and then half a step back again.

14

'Your mother rang me,' he said, 'and asked if you could stay at our house for the night.'

'Oh.'

Fidge would rather have slept in the hospital car park than go to Uncle Simon and Auntie Ruth's, but she knew that there was no point in arguing so she stood and followed her uncle along the corridor and watched him carefully spray and wipe the call button on the lift, before pressing it.

'We can't risk bringing hospital infections back to the house,' he said. 'Graham's only just over a severe sore throat and he's developed a fear of eating anything except organic ice cream.'

The lift arrived and they got in.

'Awful thing to have happened to Minnie,' he said. 'Roads are such a danger. It reminds me of when Graham fell off his bicycle, the first time he tried to ride without stabilizers. He grazed his knee and it affected him very, very badly – he wouldn't look at a picture of a bicycle for months afterwards, and we couldn't even use the word "bicycle" in conversation because if we did he'd get terribly upset and start shouting at us. In the end, we had to get him an electric scooter and a full set of body pads.'

They got out of the lift.

'We're thinking of having a lift installed at home because Graham won't use the stairs any longer – he tripped last month and now he says that every time he sets foot on a step, he can visualize himself falling head first, all the way

15

down; we've had to adapt the downstairs living room into his bedroom. His therapist says he has the most extraordinarily vivid imagination of any child she's ever met.'

They walked to the car and on the journey Uncle Simon told one Graham anecdote after another. If Mum had been there (and if it had been a normal day) she would have caught Fidge's eye, and winked. They were used to hearing about Graham in every single sentence uttered by Uncle Simon and Auntie Ruth. They knew all about how he'd been very ill as a small child, and how for months he'd had to stay away from other people, in case he caught their germs, and how he'd ended up refusing to go out at all, so that instead of going to school, he had to be taught at home. You'd think (if you'd never met him) – you'd *think*, that Graham was a tiny, delicate, sensitive creature – a sort of human butterfly, with tiny, delicate feelings to match.

You'd be wrong.

Her cousin lived in the kind of house that Fidge would have liked to live in: one completely surrounded by a garden, with an orchard and a pond. Not that Graham ever played outside. The house had five bedrooms, one of which was right in the attic, with a round window that overlooked the garden – if you put a telescope in there, you'd be able see for miles. Not that Graham had actually picked that bedroom.

As Fidge got out of her uncle's car, she saw a pale smudge looking out at her from one of the ground floor windows; it disappeared quickly as she approached.

Auntie Ruth met them at the back door, all wobbly-voiced with shock. 'How *dreadful,*' she kept saying, hugging Fidge and blinking back the tears. 'What a *dreadful* accident, poor, *poor* little Minnie.'

'Does Graham know yet?' asked Uncle Simon in a hushed voice.

Fidge's aunt nodded. 'He heard you driving off and he wanted to know what was happening. And when I told him, he was completely silent for a moment and then he asked, "Does she *have* to stay here?"' She smiled kindly over at Fidge. 'He's so sensitive to other people's feelings, you see – he knew that you wouldn't want to be away from your mother and Minnie. And then he couldn't settle afterwards, he was worried he'd have bad dreams about road accidents. I phoned his therapist and she said to try the meditation technique, so we visualized a grove of palm trees swaying in the wind, but he said that that made him think of tsunamis . . .'

The discussion continued, and Fidge sat down at the kitchen table and realized that she was incredibly hungry. She buttered and ate a slice of bread, followed by two more, and then she laid her head on her hands and went to sleep.

She woke up in a bed, and opened her eyes to see a pair of half-open curtains, and between them a sky the ominous colour of milky cocoa. Her head ached, as though a brick was resting on top of it, her teeth felt furry and she was wearing pyjamas that she'd never seen before. For a second she didn't know where she was, and then the whole dismal truth flooded through her, like a river bursting its banks, and floating on top of all the misery was a single shameful thought:

*If it wasn't for Minnie, we'd be going on holiday today.*

She sat up quickly, but she couldn't unthink the thought, and as she dressed herself in yesterday's clothes and hurried down the stairs, it kept bobbing around in her head.

'Oh, Fidge,' said Auntie Ruth, walking through the hall with a tray in her hands, 'your mother rang a while ago, but she said not to wake you – she'll call again very soon.'

'But how's Minnie?'

'Just about the same,' said Auntie Ruth, trying (and failing) to make it sound as if that were good news.

'Oh.'

Fidge stood on the stairs, without any particular reason to carry on down, or to go back up. The fact that she was neat and organized and available for emergencies was of no use to her now. She could tie knots, read instructions, scale a climbing wall, count to a hundred in Spanish and swim nearly two widths underwater, but none of this would help Minnie; there was *nothing* that she could do, apart from wish that yesterday had never happened.

'I'm just bringing Graham his mid-morning ice cream,' said Auntie Ruth, still holding the tray. 'He's halfway through a geography lesson. Why don't you join him, and I'll get you some breakfast?'

And though she didn't want to join Graham, or do geography, or eat breakfast, Fidge could think of no alternative but to unglue her feet and follow her aunt.

# FOUR

Auntie Ruth knocked tentatively on Graham's door. From behind it came a high-pitched buzzing noise that seemed to vary in volume.

After a moment or two, footsteps approached and the door was opened by a tired-looking young woman.

'Graham's just circling Lima airport,' she said. 'Apparently there's heavy cloud cover.'

A tiny model aircraft appeared briefly above her head and then zoomed away again. It crossed the enormous room, dipping down over the sofas, skimming the metre-wide computer screen, looping the loop over the bed in the shape of a racing car and finally circling the gigantic table over by the windows. Instead of a table cloth it was covered by a map of South America. The plane came steeply into land, hit the table top too hard, somersaulted off the end, and crashed into a cupboard door, snapping off both wings.

'The runway needs re-surfacing,' said Graham, dropping the remote control and picking up a small orange toy, which he immediately started fiddling with. 'My approach was perfect.'

'Do you remember how we learn?' asked the young woman, in the sort of bright voice that people normally use on toddlers. 'We learn from our *mistakes*! And in any case that wasn't Lima, that was Rio de Janeiro.'

'I didn't have enough fuel to get to Lima,' said Graham, picking up his spoon and prising a chocolate chip from the mound of ice cream in his bowl. He was large and pale, like a plant that has been heavily watered, but kept in the dark.

'This is Graham's cousin, Fidge,' said Auntie Ruth to the young woman, 'and Fidge, this is Alison, Graham's home tutor.'

'I was so sorry to hear about your sister's accident,' said Alison, gently.

Fidge, who couldn't face talking about it, nodded tightly and looked out of the window. The sky had darkened to a nasty pinkish brown and there was a faint flickering along the horizon.

'Come and sit with us,' said Alison. 'We're just discussing the Andes.'

'Actually, I've got a headache,' said Graham. 'And I feel really, really tired.'

'Oh *darling!*' exclaimed his mother, hurrying forward and placing a hand on his forehead. 'Oh dear, I wonder if we should call Dr Stevens?'

'No, I think I just need a rest,' said Graham, flopping onto one of the many sofas.

'I expect it's the high atmospheric pressure,' said Alison. 'We could have a lesson on the physics of thunderstorms.'

'No, because that would make me think about lightning strikes. I'd imagine how this house could go up in flames, or one of the trees outside could get hit and then crash through the roof and bring all the ceilings down, and this room would collapse through to the cellar so I'd be trapped in the rubble, calling helplessly while the oxygen slowly ran out.'

'I'm sure that won't happen,' said Alison.

'It might.' Graham shifted the little orange toy from hand to hand. 'You don't know, do you? It *might.*' His pale face had gone slightly blotchy.

'All right, darling,' said his mother. 'We'll finish with lessons for today. Perhaps your cousin can just stay here and play, it'll be good for both of you – oh, and I've got something to give you, Fidge,' she added. 'I shan't be a moment.'

Alison and Auntie Ruth left the room and Graham lay and fiddled with the small orange toy.

'It's a transitional object,' he said, not looking at Fidge. 'Though I don't expect you know what that means.'

'It's a plastic carrot,' said Fidge. 'On wheels.'

'It was a free gift as part of a vegetable promotion. The

22

object itself isn't important. The important thing is that it helps me to cope with change – that's what the word "transition" means – and to work through my worries.'

Fidge couldn't help giving a snort, and Graham looked at her sharply. 'Why are you laughing?' he asked.

'*What* worries? You don't have any worries.'

'Yes I do.'

'Not *real* ones.'

'What do you mean by "real"?'

'Well, what do you *think* I mean?'

She had a brief vision of Minnie lying on the road, and she tried to dispel it by turning and looking at the distant lightning again. Graham was always like this – talking as if there was something really impressive and special and marvellous about skulking indoors not doing anything. Usually when she had to spend time with him, she felt a mixture of irritation and pity. Today, though, all she felt was anger, piling up in her head so that her brain seemed to throb under the pressure.

'Real things *happen*,' she snapped. 'You spend your time *making up* stuff just so you can worry about it.'

'It feels real to me,' said Graham, his voice high and indignant. 'You have no idea what it's like to have my sort of imagination, my therapist says that it's both a gift and a curse, because I experience things much more deeply than ordinary people do.'

'Experience *what*? You don't *do* anythi—'

Fidge stopped talking as the door opened and Auntie

Ruth came in, carrying an orange plastic bag – the same bag that Uncle Simon had been holding at the hospital.

'Here we are,' she said. 'Someone picked these up and gave them to the ambulance crew. I thought they might be comforting for you to have.' She stroked Fidge's cheek, smiled at her and left.

Fidge opened the bag and her heart seemed to jolt in her chest.

Wed Wabbit stared up at her with those nasty little blackcurrant eyes. He was lying on the new pop-up edition of *The Land of Wimbley Woos* and crowded in next to him were Eleanor Elephant and the diamond-encrusted mobile phone.

Fidge's head pounded and her face felt tight and stiff. If it hadn't been for these toys, these *stupid* toys, then none of the awfulness would have happened.

If Minnie hadn't been carrying the elephant and the pathetic plastic phone, then she wouldn't have dropped Wed Wabbit. And if the Wimbley book hadn't been in the bookshop window, then Minnie wouldn't have made all that fuss and it wouldn't have been too late to get the flippers. And then Fidge wouldn't have been in a bad mood. And she wouldn't have kicked Wed Wabbit. And then Minnie wouldn't have . . . Minnie wouldn't be . . .

Rage swept through Fidge like a hurricane. She grabbed the rabbit by his red velvet ears and wrenched him out of the bag. He dangled there, long legs nearly touching the ground. She had never felt such hatred for anything in her life; she wanted to hit him, hurt him, *ruin* him. There was a rattling sound and she turned to see the windows shaking in a sudden gust. It was clear that a storm was coming, the purple clouds were bulging with rain. She ran over and pulled at the nearest window latch, already imagining Wed Wabbit lying outside in a rainstorm, blotting up the water, the way he'd done with the orange juice – she could almost see him, monstrously bloated, his seams bulging and splitting . . .

'The window's locked,' said Graham. 'In case of insects getting in. I'm not actually phobic about them, it's more that I visualize myself getting a tropical disease, something like dengue fever, or trypanosomiasis not that you'll know what either of those are.'

Fidge let go of the latch, and looked around. If she couldn't actually destroy Wed Wabbit, then she wanted to shove him away somewhere, out of her sight. From behind her came a long, low grumble of thunder. She crossed over to the cupboard door that the toy plane had crashed into, and turned the handle.

# FIVE

It wasn't a cupboard.

Fidge flicked the light switch and looked at a steep, narrow flight of stairs that led down to the right.

'It's the cellar,' said Graham. 'I have an extensive landscaped model railway down there, but I can't use stairs any more, because I tripped on a step last month and now every time I try to use them I just imagine myself—'

'I know, I know, I *know*,' interrupted Fidge. 'Your dad told me.'

She flicked off the switch again and lifted up Wed Wabbit. He seemed to be sneering at her, his expression more smug than ever. Grabbing his legs in one hand and his ears in the other, she tied him into a fierce knot and then, with a grunt of effort – like a tennis player smashing an ace – she hurled him into the darkness. The headache that had gripped her skull seemed to ease just a little. She reached into the bag again and this time threw Eleanor Elephant down the stairs, followed by the phone and the book and then she slammed the door again.

She turned to see Graham standing just behind her, twiddling the plastic carrot and looking shocked.

'Those are your *sister's* transitional objects,' he said, reprovingly, 'and she'll probably need them to cope with everything she's going through.'

'Oh shut up,' said Fidge, wearily. 'I don't want to talk about it.'

'Well, you should, it's important to share your feelings.'

'Why? You share yours the entire time and it hasn't done you much good.'

There was another low growl of thunder; the air in the room felt thick and soupy.

'My mother says . . .' began Graham, with a knowing expression.

'What?'

'My mother says that *your* mother says that since your father died you won't give anyone a hug, not even her, and she thinks you've become emotionally stunted.'

Fidge gave a gasp, as if she'd been punched. 'She didn't. She never said that.'

'Well, she mightn't have used that exact phrase, but what she meant was—'

Something seemed to explode in Fidge's head; she lunged forward and grabbed the plastic carrot, and then she spun round, wrenched open the cellar door again and threw it into the dark.

Graham stood with his mouth open, gazing at his empty hands and for a split second, the entire room turned a brilliant blueish white. A vast rumbling followed, as if a barrel had been rolled from one side of the sky to the other. Distantly, a phone rang.

'I need it back,' said Graham, his voice a squeak. 'I can't survive a storm without my transitional object.'

Fidge had never felt as angry as she did now; her whole body was shaking, and the world seemed to jump around in front of her eyes.

'Go and get it then,' she said, and her voice sounded flat and cruel.

'I can't.'

'You've got legs, haven't you?'

Distantly, came the sound of Auntie Ruth calling Fidge's name.

'Fetch it for me,' ordered Graham.

'Fetch it yourself, you're not a baby. Or actually – maybe you are.'

'I'm not.'

'Maybe you don't need a trans-thingy object, maybe you need a *dummy*.'

'It's "transitional". You can't even say the word properly.'

'*I* don't need to. *I* can walk downstairs like a normal ten-year-old.'

'Fidge!' called Auntie Ruth. 'It's your mum on the phone.'

'Mum?' As Fidge sprinted from the room, there was another brilliant flash, and a great rip of thunder, nearer and louder than the last. She glanced back to see Graham standing as if stapled to the spot.

'Fidge!' said her mother, and the word was full of energy, and Fidge knew straight away that it was better news. 'Minnie's woken up! She's pretty sore and miserable, but she's woken up and she's asking where you are and you'll never guess what else she's asking for.'

'What?' asked Fidge.

'Wed Wabbit. She keeps demanding to see Wed Wabbit, over and over and over again.' Her mother was half-laughing, half-tearful. 'So you've got to bring him in, Auntie Ruth says she'll drive you here after lunch, and I can't wait to see you, oh I can't wait . . .'

Fidge closed her eyes and then opened them; in thirty seconds the world had changed. She felt as if she'd been swimming in deep murky water, and had just broken surface into the light. Minnie was awake. Minnie was awake and she needed Fidge to do something for her! She took a huge breath and managed to smile at her aunt.

'I've got to get something,' she said, and she ran back to Graham's room.

The sky outside was as dark as twilight.

'Graham!' she shouted; she couldn't see him anywhere in the room. 'Look, I'm sorry, OK. I shouldn't have thrown your transitional thing down the stairs, I'll go and get it.'

There was no answer. Fidge went over to the cellar door; as she approached she could hear a whimpering sound.

The light was on. The toys lay in a cluster at the bottom of the stairs, the pink lights on the phone still twinkling, the carrot-on-wheels resting on the top, but Graham was nowhere near them. He was standing just three steps down, pressed against the wall, his face the colour of skimmed milk.

'I keep imagining . . .' he said, his voice barely audible. 'I keep imagining that I'll fall, and then something even worse – something totally terrible – will happen to me.'

'I'll get it for you,' said Fidge, hurrying down, but he grabbed her arm as she passed him, and held on.

'Honestly, it's OK,' said Fidge. 'Just go back up again. I have to get Wed Wabbit as well, it's really, really important.' She could see the knotted-up shape of Minnie's toy, its body partly covered by the new copy of *The Land of Wimbley Woos*, its ears folded down over its face, so that only one eye was visible.

'I can't,' said Graham.

'Why not?' She tried to unpeel his fingers but they were clamped immovably round her bicep.

'Something huge is going to happen,' he said, his voice a scared whisper. 'The atmosphere's full of static electricity. Can't you feel it?'

And Fidge realized that she *could* feel it; her hair was trying to stand upright and the air felt almost too thick to breathe. 'It's only the storm,' she said, still trying to pull herself away, but afraid of unbalancing him. From the bottom of the stairs, Wed Wabbit's one visible eye gazed grimly up at her.

'Let me *go*, Graham.'

'But there's going to be the worst—'

Graham's sentence ended in a gasp, as a soundless sword-thrust of light sliced past the half-open door and down the stairs, so brilliant that the shape of Wed Wabbit's head stayed imprinted on Fidge's eyes, outlined in a sliding, fizzing green, and then there was a thunder clap, vast and sudden, like a giant stamping on the house.

And then utter darkness.

# SIX

Graham had gone. His hands were no longer squeezing her arm. Fidge's first thought was that he'd fallen down the cellar stairs and she yelled his name into the darkness, and heard, to her cold amazement, her voice disappearing into the distance, as if she were standing in a vast hall instead of a narrow staircase. She shifted slightly, and felt the crunch of small stones underfoot, and at the same time she heard a noise behind her – a noise that was both familiar and yet also wildly, hugely *wrong*.

DIDDLY DUM, DIDDLY DUM, DIDDLY DUM, DIDDLY DUM, DIDDLY DUM,

# DIDDLY DUM, DIDDLY DUM, DIDDLY DUM, DIDDLY DUM

She turned, catching her foot on a metal rail, and saw two round orange lights that grew rapidly, and there was a crescendo of sound —

# DIDDLY DUM, DIDDLY DUM, DIDDLY DUM, DIDDLY DUM, DIDDLY DUM

— and she leaped clumsily aside as a steam train hurtled by – a hammering roar, a blur of smoke, a streak of light, and then it was gone, leaving only the battering wind of its passing. Fidge stood again in darkness, her body pressed against the wall.

'I'm dreaming,' she said out loud, but her shoulder hurt where she'd banged it on the wall and her eyes stung from the smoke, so she couldn't be dreaming, and she wasn't dead either, unless dead people can feel their ears popping. Not dreaming then, and not dead, but *somewhere else* – somewhere else and on her own.

'Graham?' she called, and when he didn't answer, she felt the tiniest shred of disappointment because even Graham would have been better than nothing. 'Mum?' she shouted. 'Minnie?' And then – just because it was good to hear the word – 'Dad?'

And when (of course) there was no reply, she started walking in the same direction that the train had travelled in, trailing one hand along the wall, using every speck of her willpower in order to remain calm. It was only a couple of minutes before she saw the pale, green-smudged semicircle of the tunnel mouth far ahead and she had nearly reached it and had watched the green smudges turn into steep-sided grassy banks when the rails began to hum and she heard the noise of another train behind her.

She began to run, her feet crunching on the gravel in the same rhythm as the engine, and she reached daylight just in front of the train, and dodged to one side, into the long grass at the base of the embankment. The train hurtled past, puffing neat little balls of smoke. Its engine was a glossy black and the carriages bottle green, with brass fittings. The whole thing shone as if it had been painted and polished ten minutes before, but it wasn't the newness of the train that left Fidge staring; it was the glimpse of the passengers. They'd sped by too fast for her to see them properly, but the impression she had was of . . . greyness. Total greyness, without a single speck of colour.

The noise of the train dwindled into the distance and there was silence apart from the shrill scrape of grasshoppers. Overhead, the sky was bright blue, criss-crossed by swallows. Fidge tried to climb up the side of the bank but it was too steep and the grass too short to hang on to. After a moment of hesitation, she jumped down and carried on walking along the track; her footsteps seemed very loud.

She had been walking for nearly five minutes, her mind a determined blank, when yet again she heard the noise of a train. This time she turned to see it approach; it was the same colour as the last one, the brass-work brilliant in the sunlight, the passengers the same blur of featureless grey, but as it passed, she saw something white fly out of a window and dance in the train's wake. It landed between the rails, far ahead, and she ran to pick it up: a piece of paper, crumpled into a tight ball. It took her a while to smooth it out enough to read the pencilled message.

Three times now we've seen you, stranger,
Can you help us in our danger –
Turn our land to joy from pain
And likewise get us off this train?

If you'll accept our desperate plea
Then grateful we'll for ever be
Your task will need brains, brawn and heart,
First find the Purples: that's the start.

Fidge frowned. 'First find the *what*?' A terrible and extraordinary thought began signalling from the back of her brain, but she chose to ignore it. She pocketed the message and then – since there was nothing else to do – carried on walking. The embankments on either side were getting lower and she began to jog along the track, eager to escape from this claustrophobic path and find a wider view. Ahead, she could see some bushes growing up one of the slopes, and she broke into a sprint and – still at speed – swerved up the bank, grabbing at branches to help her, and emerged at the top, breathless.

And saw something impossible.

# SEVEN

'No,' said Fidge. But saying the word didn't change anything. The rolling green landscape with trees the shape of lollipops stayed the same and the villages of striped and spotted houses and the single bottle-green train rushing round what was obviously a circular track.

Most of all it didn't change the cylindrical pink figure rushing towards her with its arms outstretched. Fidge turned and hared back down the embankment, yelling, but the train was coming round again and she barely managed to cross the rails before it thundered by. She started climbing up the opposite bank but there were no handholds and as the last carriage whipped past, she turned in despair and saw the Pink Wimbley Woo – *because that, without a shadow of a doubt, was what it was* – waving to her from the other side of the track. It was about the size of an adult human, but an adult human in the shape of a barrel, with short, bendy arms and legs, large eyes that looked painted on – *except that they blinked* – a blob for a nose, and a large mouth, which was currently stretched in a smile that covered about a quarter of the cylindrical body. The overall effect was horrible.

'Go away,' said Fidge, backing off. Out of the corner of her eye, she could see another balled-up piece of paper, bouncing along the gravel.

The Wimbley bent over and picked up the paper, its whole body tipping in one piece, hinged at the hip. It had, Fidge noticed, four fingers on each hand; all of them seemed to be made of rubber.

'Oooh look —' said the Wimbley, unfolding the note; its
    voice was high yet burbling, like a mouse gargling
    treacle. '— this letter's meant for you,
So read it, new friend, read it do.'

Still smiling hugely, it held the paper out to Fidge. She hesitated for a moment and then leaned forward very slightly so that she could see what was written. It was another poem.

A fourth time seen, a second plea
Please, stranger, set the Wimblies free

Us Greys must place our trust in you
To take this quest and see it through.
For though we are the Wimbley brain
We've been imprisoned on the train.

Seek out the Purples, they possess
The secret that will solve this mess
But if you're needing help or news
Please don't rely on other hues.
The Orange, Yellow, Green or Pink
Have no ability to think
And of the Blues we dare not speak
For with their strength they crush the weak.

Fidge took a step back and looked at the Pink Wimbley again; it certainly looked brainless. And harmless. Before she could stop them, some lines from Minnie's book slid into her head:

*Yellow are timid, Blue are strong,*
*Grey are wise and rarely wrong,*
*Green are daring, Pink give cuddles . . .*

'That's *enough*,' she said firmly, more to herself than to the Wimbley. 'What I need to do is get back home to Mum and Minnie. Before I go completely mad.'

The Pink Wimbley stretched out its arms for a hug, one

hand still clutching the note.

'No,' said Fidge, flinching at the thought.

'But if you're feeling tired or sad
A lovely hug will make you glad.'

'No it won't.'

'A hug a day is so much fun
A hug an hour suits everyone!'

'Please,' said Fidge, 'just *go away.*'

The enormous smile disappeared, to be replaced by a slightly sulky expression.

'All right then, I'll go ahead
And hug someone who's *kind* instead.'

'Yes, you do that,' muttered Fidge.

The Wimbley swivelled rather huffily, and retraced its route up the scrubby bank. At the top, it turned round, hesitated and then hopefully held out its arms again.

'No,' said Fidge.

The Wimbley turned again and disappeared from view.

Fidge closed her eyes tightly.

'I have to get out of here,' she said, concentrating hard, trying not to think of where 'here' might be – trying instead to visualize normal things, like Minnie's toy-strewn side of the bedroom, and the scorched brown patch on the living-room carpet dating from when Mum had dropped the iron.

'I *have* to get out of here. Right now.' She waited. The grasshoppers shrilled in unison.

'Right now,' she repeated. The grasshoppers were joined by the distant sound of the train coming round again.

'Right n—'

Her eyes snapped open. A terrible warbling shriek was coming from the other side of the embankment, and it was followed by the tremulous voice of the Pink Wimbley.

'Please loose my arms and let me go
Whose note this is I do not know,
I simply found it by the track—'

'You're lying,' came a shouted reply – a thicker, deeper
        voice, 'you'll be coming back
With us – unless you tell us who
This stranger is in Wimbley Woo.'

The Pink shrieked again:

'I can't, because I do not know
Her name – *ow!*'

'Hang on,' shouted Fidge, starting to scramble up the

bushy slope. 'What are you doing?' But her voice was drowned under the noise of the passing train, and then an entire shrub came away in her hand and she slithered back down to the trackside in a shower of earth. She toiled up again, all ready to launch herself at whoever was hurting the ridiculous pink object, and then stopped in shock, mid-stride, her head just poking over the top of the embankment.

The entire field below her was filled with Blue Wimblies. They were standing to attention, drawn up in columns like an army; each was tall and bulky with weirdly muscled arms and legs; each wore a red sash around its middle. Through their midst, the Pink Wimbley was being forcibly led away.

'A hug?' it was suggesting, feebly. 'Because I'd like to say
A hug will always make your day
So if you're cross or if you're sad
A hug's the thing to make you gl— *urk*.'

The end of the word was cut off, as a sash was firmly tied around its mouth.

'Atten*shun* troops,' shouted a Blue who, unlike the others,
    was wearing a maroon beret. 'We'll split in two
And scour the land of Wimbley Woo.
An uninvited stranger's here
And our Blue Wimbley task is clear:
Search every house, search every farm . . .'

It paused, and the next words were roared out by everyone in the field apart from the gagged prisoner:

'AND KEEP OUR LEADER SAFE FROM HARM!'

Fidge crouched in the undergrowth and watched the Blues forming into units, feet thudding on the turf. They were well drilled, their expressions fixed and severe and despite the fact that they were basically just large blue dustbins, the sheer size and number of them was actually menacing. In fact the whole situation felt quite . . . Fidge groped for the right word and to her dismay came up with 'real'. She *really* didn't want to get caught. She was *really* quite frightened. And she *really* felt worried about what was going to happen to the Pink Wimbley. She could still see it, being marched away along a lane between two guards, and the word '-Ug' was faintly audible, borne on the breeze.

The two halves of the Blue army fanned out in opposite directions, moving rapidly. Fidge waited five minutes, until the nearest of the soldiers was just a blue dot, and then slithered down the embankment into the field and scampered towards the nearest hedge. Walking in a crouch, she found her way to the gate, and then into the lane where she'd last seen the prisoner and its escorts. She broke into a cautious trot and headed after them

# EIGHT

Meanwhile, Graham was sitting on a hilltop, watching a yellow butterfly waver past. The grass beneath him was soft and springy and dotted with white daisies, the air smelled fresh, and the sky was a brilliant blue. At the base of the hill, a sunlit landscape of fields and hedgerows stretched to the horizon, dotted with brightly coloured houses. Somewhere a train whistle blew.

Of course, Graham wasn't *really* sitting there – he was just imagining the whole thing. He was certain about that, partly because he never went outdoors these days, so it *couldn't* be real – and partly because parked next to him was a human-sized plastic carrot. It was mounted on small orange wheels and had the words MADE IN CHINA stamped on the back.

'I do hope that the grass is not damp,' remarked the carrot, in a brisk, no-nonsense sort of voice.

'It's not,' said Graham. He was feeling wonderfully relaxed; one moment he'd been trying to rescue his transitional object in the middle of a violent electrical storm and in the aggressive presence of his boringly average cousin, and the next he was in this peaceful, beautiful world conjured up by his own, quite remarkable, imagination.

'It certainly looks damp,' continued the carrot. 'And if it *is* damp then you are simply storing up problems for the years ahead. When you find yourself hobbling along on two sticks, groaning with pain, perhaps you will think back and say, "Oh, how I wish I had listened to Doctor Carrot, she was absolutely right about the grass".'

'*Doctor* Carrot?' echoed Graham, contemptuously. 'You're not a doctor. You were a free gift from the supermarket.'

'I will thank you not to contradict me, young man. If you look on my base you will see my title clearly marked.'

Graham peered at the small platform to which the carrot was fixed, and saw some lettering.

## DR VEG PROM CARROT

He snorted. 'The "DR" doesn't mean doctor, it's short for "Douglas Retail" – that's the name of the shop I got you from. And "veg prom" is just an abbreviation for "vegetable promotion".'

Grinning, he glanced up at the carrot. She had very small features – spots for eyes and a mouth that was just a horizontal crease. The crease was not smiling back. After a moment or two, the carrot's wheels started moving; she manoeuvred back and forth a couple of times, like a car performing a three-point turn, until she was angled slightly away from Graham. Silence fell.

Graham turned back to admire the view. It had changed slightly. A line of blue dots had appeared in the field immediately below the hilltop and he watched it for a while, wondering what his amazing imagination had come up with now. The dots seemed to be moving up the hill towards him.

'What do you think those are?' he asked. 'Are they symbolic of something? A worry or a fear?'

There was no reply from the carrot.

The blue dots seemed to have *legs*.

'I said, "what do you think those are?"' repeated Graham, more sharply; he wasn't used to being ignored. He was also beginning to feel the usual fear sliding back under his skin, like a trickle of cold water. It was a sensation he lived with most of the time, and the fact that he'd just spent ten minutes without it, made its return all the more horrible.

'I don't like this,' said Graham and his voice sounded scratchy with nerves. 'Talk to me.'

The carrot didn't speak or turn round, and from the hunch of her shoulders (or whatever you called the top bit of a carrot) it was obvious that she was sulking.

Graham stood up, his mouth dry. The blue dots were

making noises, were moving faster. He thought he could hear one of them shouting the word 'stranger'. He glanced around and saw that there was a steep track behind him leading down the other side of the hill, but it disappeared into a belt of dense woodland, and he was scared of trees, with their creaking branches, and rustling leaves, and shadowy hollows. He couldn't possibly go into the forest alone.

'Hey,' he said to the carrot. 'We need to go. Come *on*.' And when, yet again, there was no answer, Graham realized with a sinking of the heart what he had to do. Something awful. Something utterly pointless and painful.

'OK,' he said. 'I'm *sorry*, right?'

The wheels shifted slightly.

'I'm sorry, *Dr Carrot*,' came the clipped voice.

'I'm sorry, Dr Carrot.'

'I'm sorry, Dr Carrot, that I was rude and that I scoffed at your medical qualifications.'

'I'm sorry, Dr Carrot, that I was rude' – Graham glanced over his shoulder and the blue dots had now become running blue cylinders with eyes. 'Come *on*, we have to get away!' he screamed.

'And that I scoffed at your medical qualifications,' repeated the carrot, grimly.

'AndthatIscoffedatyourmedicalqualifications. Please! *Please!*'

'Apology accepted, although I felt it lacked a certain sincerity. Now, I believe that you wanted to discuss whether the blue objects approaching us are symbolic of something.'

'No no no no no, please, not now.' Graham was almost jumping up and down with anxiety.

'It's an interesting idea.'

'*It isn't*, it's *boring*! We have to *go*!!!' He couldn't bear to look back at the pursuers with their fixed staring eyes and bulging arms and painted mouths that were shouting something that he was too terrified to understand.

'We'll postpone it then.' Dr Carrot wheeled round, and started heading the other way. 'Climb on.'

Graham took a clumsy step onto the wheeled base, wrapped his arms around the orange body and closed his eyes. From behind him there were shouts, but they were soon lost under the sound of the wind whipping past his ears as they hurtled down the slope towards the wood.

Dr Carrot shouted something that Graham couldn't hear.

'*What?*' he asked.

'Need to *brake*.'

'Where is it?'

'What?'

'The *brake*.'

'There isn't one.'

'What?'

'Foot.'

'What?'

'Use your *foot*.'

'How?'

The reply was lost in the whistle of air. Graham, who

**48**

had never sledged – or even freewheeled on a bike – thought briefly about sticking out a foot and then thought for slightly longer about catching that foot on a root and breaking his leg in multiple places and ending up on crutches with a metal knee. He kept the foot where it was, closed his eyes and hung on.

The wheels hit a bump and for a moment, he and Dr Carrot were flying.

And then they weren't.

Graham lay on the ground and gazed upward at the branches of an enormous tree and at its shifting canopy of leaves. Needles of sunlight pierced the gaps.

He tried to take a breath, but there seemed to be no space for air in his lungs; he felt as flat as a piece of paper. From his right came a squeaking noise, and Dr Carrot jerked gradually into vision. She was leaning sideways at a peculiar angle.

Graham flapped his mouth a couple of times, but nothing came out but a thin wheeze.

'You're winded,' said Dr Carrot. 'You landed flat on your back. Give yourself ten minutes and you'll be as right as rain.'

'Need an ambulance,' mouthed Graham.

'I don't think we want to waste valuable hospital time on a minor injury, do we?'

'Yes.'

'My front axle mounting is severely bent, but you don't notice *me* calling for medical attention, do you?'

'You're a carrot,' mouthed Graham. 'They don't have hospitals for carrots.'

The thin mouth grew thinner. There was a pause and then Dr Carrot jerked squeakily out of view again.

Graham stared up at the shifting leaves and wondered if it would be possible to sue Dr Carrot. There'd be a long list of possible charges: driving without brakes, failure to install seatbelts, reckless endangerment of a minor . . .

Above him, a section of leafy shadow seemed to move. He frowned up at it. The shadow moved again, and was joined by a second and suddenly they were dropping towards him, steadily and smoothly like spiders on silken threads and Graham tried to scream, but only managed a pathetic rattle as a large green hand was clamped over his mouth.

# NINE

Fidge kept to a slow jog. The lane had high hedges and was ridiculously, endlessly wiggly, like a child's drawing of a snake, and she was worried that she might turn a corner and suddenly crash into the guards and their Pink prisoner. If it came to a fight with a Blue Wimbley she was sure she'd lose.

She searched around in her head for something else she could be sure about: somewhere in the back of her mind a seed of panic was beginning to sprout, and she knew that the best way to stop it from growing was to slap a great pile of *facts* on top of it. 'The more you know, the less you fear', her dad had always said, when he'd talked about being a fireman. Fidge didn't understand what was happening to her, or why it was happening, or how (or if, or when, or where, for that matter) but the best way she could think of to cope was by behaving as if she were an explorer who had just been parachuted into a strange but solid land; an explorer who'd luckily happened to read the guidebook eight million times before setting out.

'*Fact*,' she said, out loud. 'I'm in the Land of Wimbley Woos.' It was reassuring to hear her own voice, even if it wasn't quite as firm as usual. '*Fact*: Yellows are timid, Blues are strong and Greys are wise and rarely wrong. *Fact*: Green are daring, Pink give cuddles, Orange are silly and get in muddles. *Fact*: Purple Wimblies understand the past and future of their land. *Fact*: something's gone wrong here and I need to free the Pink and get the whole thing sorted out as quickly as possible. Because I *have* to get home and see my sister. And I *have* to bring her Wed—'

She came to a sudden halt. Ahead of her lay a crossroads. Parked beside a signpost was a bicycle and trailer with the word TAXI written across it; two Orange Wimblies were standing in the trailer, while a Yellow Wimbley knelt beside the bike, pumping up the back tyre. All three swivelled to look at Fidge, their eyes huge and unblinking.

'—Wabbit,' she said, finishing her sentence.

The Yellow let out a thin scream, dropped the bicycle pump, and hared off along one of the leafy lanes, its cry of distress slowly fading.

The Oranges stared at her open-mouthed.

'Don't be scared,' said Fidge. 'I won't do you any harm. Did you see which way the Blues went?'

There was a very long pause and then one of the Oranges began to giggle – an idiotic bleat that set Fidge's teeth on edge.

'Did you see which way the Blues went?' she repeated, with just a hint of impatience.

'I saw them go in that direction,' said the non-giggler, indicating left.

'Or, actually,' it continued, turning round, 'maybe on reflection,

They might have gone towards the Square.'

'No, no,' said the other Orange, sticking out an arm. 'They headed over *there*.'

Fidge looked from one of them to the other – they were actually pointing in *opposite directions*. 'You can't have forgotten already,' she said. 'They had a prisoner with them. A Pink.'

There was another very long pause and then *both* of the Oranges began to giggle.

'Please,' she said, walking towards them. 'It's important. Try to think really hard and—'

She stumbled over the dropped bicycle pump. It was just a minor trip, nothing spectacular, but the Oranges reacted as if they'd just seen the funniest thing in the entire history of the universe: hooting with laughter, doubling-up, leaning against each other, holding their stomachs, *weeping*.

'Oh for heaven's sake,' muttered Fidge, as the hysteria went on and on. She circled the signpost, looking up at what was written on each of the four arms.

WIMBLEY STATION
WIMBLEY FAIR
WIMBLEY TOURIST INFORMATION OFFICE
WIMBLEY SQUARE

Then she positioned herself right underneath it, jumped up and managed to grab one of the arms. For a few seconds she dangled by one hand, craning all around, and just as her fingers began to lose their grip she saw a flash of blue above one of the hedgerows. She dropped down and tore after it, the sound of silliness dwindling behind her.

'*Fact*,' panted Fidge, to herself, 'Oranges are a total waste of space.'

It wasn't long before the lane ended, abruptly and unexpectedly, on the edge of a town square. Fidge suddenly found herself out in the open. She ducked down behind a nearby bench and peered between the slats at the view: it was quite pretty, in a grandma's-birthday-card sort of way. The square was lined with shops, the buildings curvy and painted in pale pinks and greens, as if carved out of melting ice cream, and there was a garden in the centre, surrounding a very tall column, topped with a statue. Blossoming trees lined the road, butterflies danced above the flower beds, robins twittered and on the far side of the square, a Blue Wimbley snapped a pair of handcuffs onto the wrists of the gagged Pink, and shoved it into the back of a truck.

# TEN

The truck door slammed. Fidge tensed in her hiding place, waiting for a chance to gallop to the rescue, but the Blue Wimbley stayed beside the vehicle and jogged on the spot for a minute or two, before starting on some vigorous press-ups. The Pink stared out of the window, blinking pathetically.

It was an odd sort of truck: the bit at the back where the Pink Wimbley was imprisoned was separated from the driver's seat by two pairs of bicycles, fixed together, one pair behind the other. The driver's door had a large picture of a cupcake painted on it but someone had crudely daubed the words **PRISONER TRANSPORT** over the top of it, in dark red.

The same paint had been used to write **POLICE HEADQUARTERS** across the window of a baker's shop, right next to where the truck was parked.

As Fidge watched, trying to decide what to do, the shop door burst open, and four Yellow Wimblies hurtled out onto the pavement, closely followed by another Blue who was holding a stick in one hand and a paper bag in the other.

The Blue with the stick shouted harshly and the Yellows swarmed towards the truck and climbed onto the bicycles. Both Blues got into the front and one of them turned round, puffed into the paper bag and then burst it with a loud bang. The Yellows screamed, their legs started pedalling and the truck quickly picked up speed, travelled part way around the square and then exited along a side road. Fidge could see the Pink in the back, its eyes pressed hopelessly against the window, the red gag like a wound across its face.

The birds continued to sing in the blossoming trees, but their song sounded hollow and thin. The prettiness felt painted on; nasty things were happening here.

Fidge edged out from behind the bench, keeping her eye on the Police Headquarters. The door stayed closed; nothing moved in the window; nothing moved in the whole of the square apart from the birds and butterflies. She darted halfway across, taking shelter behind the broad base of the column at the centre of the garden. She was just about to sprint after the truck – though with no real hope of catching it – when she noticed a handle protruding from the stone-work. She gave it an experimental tug and a door swung open, revealing the bottom of a spiral staircase. Hesitating, she took a step back and gazed upward, realizing for the first time that there was a railing around the statue at the top.

She took the stairs at a run and emerged, breathless, onto a terrace, far above the rooftops of the town square. Stretching to the horizon on all sides lay Wimbley Land, looking just as it had in Minnie's book: fields of poppies and woods of vivid green, houses as brightly decorated as birthday cakes, a giant wheel somewhere in the distance, with a cluster of bright-pink lights twinkling just beside it, and a nearby conical hill topped by a flag-festooned castle and surrounded by a water-filled moat.

She could see the steam train, still hurtling round its circular track, and she could see the truck, speeding in the direction of the castle, the pedalling Yellows bent low over the handlebars. She watched it until it disappeared behind a clump of trees and then another movement caught her eye: a troop of Blues, marching in formation across a nearby field. Slowly, she walked around the perimeter of the terrace and spotted a second group of Blues knocking at the door of a farmhouse, while a third set up a roadblock on the lane that led to the castle.

They seemed to be everywhere. *What could she do?* The minutes were ticking away, and Minnie was waiting for her, Minnie was relying on her, but where could she even *begin*?

She had a sudden thought, and reached into her pocket for the note that had been flung from the train.

If you'll accept our desperate plea
Then grateful we'll for ever be
Your task will need brains, brawn and heart,
First find the Purples: that's the start.

'Right,' said Fidge, snatching at this small instruction, like a climber grabbing onto a firm handhold. 'So what I need to do is find some Purples.'

She turned to descend, and saw an inscription carved on the stonework in front of her.

### GOOD KING WIMBLEY
### FAIR AND TRUE,
### HE'S EVERY COLOUR
### AND EVERY HUE

Above the writing stood a large stone statue of a crowned Wimbley, its expression calm and noble.

'Well, you're not doing a very good job,' said Fidge, severely. 'This place seems about as unfair as it's possible to be.' And then she ran back down the staircase, pausing at the bottom to peer round the edge of the door. Her caution was justified: two Blues were leaving the Police Headquarters. They marched halfway across the square, feet smacking the pavement, and then came to a sudden halt in front of an empty sweet shop. The words CLOSED UNTIL FURTHER NOTICE were pasted across the window.

Fidge crouched in the shadows, waiting for them to leave; she had half an idea about where to start her hunt for the Purples, but it meant returning to the crossroads, and the Blues were just beside the exit road she needed.

A minute went by, then another – and then another. Strangely, the Blues stayed put; they were gazing through the sweet-shop window at the empty shelves, their faces pressed against the glass.

Slowly, warily, Fidge stood up. Not taking her eyes from the Wimblies, she tiptoed across the square, scarcely daring to breathe as she passed behind them.

They didn't look round; they were too busy talking in their thick, sinister, gurgling voices.

About sweets.

'I miss the lemon bonbons most,' said the first Blue.
'I miss marshmallow fluff on toast,' replied the second.
'I got rewarded yesterday
And chose a giant Milky Way,' said the first.
'*I've* been to the Rewards Room twice
And both times I picked chocolate mice,' said the other.
'White chocolate?'
'Yes. But now I wish
I'd gone for cola fizzy fish.'

The discussion moved on to gobstoppers and Fidge, to her astonishment, was able to edge past unnoticed. She paused at the mouth of the lane, heard the words 'sherbet makes my tongue feel weird' and took to her heels.

It didn't take long to get back to the crossroads. To her relief, the Oranges and their taxi had gone; Fidge checked the signpost for the destination she wanted, and then hurried onwards.

# ELEVEN

Graham was in a tree. He was sitting on a wide platform, his back against the trunk, and if he opened his eyes, he could see the ground about ten metres below. Mainly, though, he was keeping them shut. There was a strong wind, and the platform was swaying slightly.

'I'm going to die,' he said. 'Get me down immediately. *Immediately.*'

There was a squeaky, ratcheting noise just to his left.

'Thank you very much indeed,' said Dr Carrot.

Graham opened his eyes a crack, and saw a large green dustbin kneeling beside the carrot's wheeled base. The dustbin had arms and legs. And eyes. And a voice – a great, booming, hearty, eardrum-denting voice.

'I've glued it but the axle's split
You'll soon need much more work on it.'

'Nevertheless,' said Dr Carrot, 'it's a considerable improvement.'

'So now you're fit you'll join our band
To bring peace back to Wimbley Land?'

'Can you keep the noise down?' asked Graham. 'I have very sensitive hearing.'

'I see myself as more of an adviser than a fighter,' said Dr Carrot, 'but perhaps I can venture one or two tips on strategy.'

'This carrot here will join our throng!
Let's sing our rousing freedom song.'

'No, let's not,' began Graham, 'because I'm beginning to get a head—'

The rest of the word 'headache' was drowned out by a massed chorus of green cylinders, some abseiling down ropes, others roaring from the canopies of nearby trees, still others leaping onto the platform from higher branches, making the whole structure shudder terrifyingly.

'Our country's hour of peril's here
Our patriotic duty's clear

We have to swing from tree to tree
To save us all from tyranny.
Wimbley Woo, Wimbley Woo
We'll leap and run and climb for you,
We'll jump, ski, swim, surf, skateboard too
To save our glorious Wimbley Woo!'

As the last, thunderous note died away, another noise could be heard – gruff shouts and running feet, coming from the forest floor. Graham risked a quick look down and saw a swarm of Blue figures, all pointing up towards the tree-top platform. The green dustbins gaped back, seemingly amazed.

'The guards – they've somehow found our nest!'

'Because, *obviously*, they heard you shouting,' said Graham.

'We'll have to flee. Quick, head south west.'

'And now they'll have heard that too. Well done.'

'The young man has a point,' said Dr Carrot. 'Though he's expressed it rather rudely. Perhaps another direction would be preferable.'

'Yes, let's confuse our blue-tinged foe

Come one, come all, we'll NORTHWARDS go.'

'Don't you *get* it?' asked Graham, as – ten metres below – the Blue guards all nodded at each other and turned northwards. 'If you'd just stop yelling the entire—'

The next second, he was scooped up, tucked into a huge net bag and slung over a Green's shoulder, and found himself swooping nauseatingly through the tree-tops on a series of rope swings. The Green who was carrying him did a complete somersault at one point, for no apparent reason, and Graham screamed as the leafy world spun around him. By the time the bag was set down, on yet another lofty platform, he was limp with terror, unable even to sit up, every muscle trembling.

Dr Carrot rolled over to him. 'How are you feeling?' she asked.

'Get me home. Now.'

'I think somebody needs to learn the word "please".'

'You can't expect me to be polite when I'm under extreme psychological stress.'

The carrot's little black eyes studied him thoughtfully. If she'd had hands, she would have been stroking her chin. If she'd had a chin. 'And what aspects of the current situation are making you so uneasy?'

'Oh goodness, let me think,' said Graham, sarcastically. 'Well, how about the fact that I've been hurled into a strange country, thrown around in mid-air by a crowd of shouting bins and I'm talking to a *carrot*?' His voice was shaking and he turned away so that he didn't have to look at her, and instead fixed his eyes on a section of tree trunk. He focused on the rigid brown swirls, trying to push away the whole hideous outdoor world that surrounded him.

'Now that's an interesting metaphor,' said Dr Carrot.

'What is?'

'You're concentrating on the small view directly in front of you, whereas I was going to suggest that looking at the broader picture might ease your anxiety. On our recent journey between trees I was discussing the history of Wimbley Land with the green gentleman who was carrying me. This country has historically been ruled by a monarchy, which means there was a king on the throne—'

'Yes, I know what the word "monarchy" means. I have an IQ of over a hundred and sixty.'

'In that case I'd expect you also to know the definition of "manners".'

There was a moment of silence.

'As I was saying,' continued Dr Carrot, 'there was a king on the throne and all was peace and harmony until a recent coup, a word which means—'

'Coup,' interrupted Graham. 'A violent or illegal change in government.'

'Precisely. So instead of Good King Wimbley fair and true, they now have a dictator who is making things rather unpleasant for all concerned, and is protected by the Blue guards.

The Greens have formed what you might call a rebel army.'

'I don't care.'

'They're planning to storm the castle.'

'I said I don't care. I hate this place, whatever it is. *Where* ever it is. I want to go home.' He could hear the group of Greens bellowing on the other side of the platform; their conversation had to be audible for miles. It wouldn't be long before the Blues arrived yet again, and then he'd be shoved into a bag and whirled around and the thought of it made him feel ill. 'I just want everything to be back to normal. You're my transitional object, you're supposed to help me cope with changes. Get me back home. Now.' He swallowed. *'Please.'* The last word came out as a desperate wail.

There was a squeak and Dr Carrot's wheels gently nudged his shoulder. When she spoke, her voice was a little less clipped, a little softer.

'So you want to go home? Back to your usual life?'

'Yes. Yes yes yes.'

'Back to living on the ground floor because you're frightened of climbing stairs?'

'Yes.'

'Back to never going into the sunshine? Never being around other children? Bad dreams? Phobias? A life behind closed curtains?'

Graham paused very slightly. 'Yes,' he said.

'And what if I told you that at present I don't actually know how to get you home.'

'Then get me off this tree. It would be a start. And then we can go and phone my parents or order a taxi or . . . or . . .' Somewhere in the back of his head lurked the thought that a land populated by abseiling dustbins was unlikely to have a phone signal. 'Or maybe I can just *think* myself back home.' He closed his eyes and tried very hard to visualize his bedroom, but his thoughts were jumping around like fleas and all he could see was the sunlight turning his eyelids red. And then the volume of the shouting went up another notch.

'The Blues have found us yet again!
Let's head towards our secret den
It's just north-east of Wimbley Fair
I'm sure they'll never find us there!'

'OK,' said Graham, scrambling to his feet. 'I'm getting off this tree. *Now.*'

# TWELVE

In front of Wimbley Tourist Information Office there was a taxi rank. Eight bicycle trailers were parked next to each other, a Yellow Wimbley standing beside each, and as Fidge approached, the Yellows edged closer and closer together until they formed a nervous, shifting clump.

'Hi,' said Fidge, awkwardly.

Eight pairs of eyes stared at her. The Yellow at the front started to speak and then panicked and elbowed its way to the back of the clump; there was a bit of shoving and nudging before the new front Wimbley cleared its throat. Its voice was wobbly with nerves.

'Hello stranger, how are you?
Welcome, please to Wimbley Woo.

We're here to help, just tell us where,
And let a taxi take you there.'

'I need to go and see the Purples,' said Fidge. 'I was going to ask the Tourist Information Office where I can find them, but maybe you can tell me?'

'The Mystic Grove. It won't take long.
Just pay me and we'll speed along.'

'But I don't have any money on me.'

'A song, a joke, a dance, a cake,
Are payments that we like to take.'

'Oh, OK. I'll tell you a joke, then. Knock Knock.'

There was a pause.

'Knock knock,' repeated Fidge. 'And now *you* say "Who's there?"'

There was another pause.

'Go on,' said Fidge. 'Say "Who's there?" otherwise I can't tell the joke.'

The Wimbley at the front shifted anxiously from foot to foot and then one of the other Yellows raised a hand.

'Yes?' said Fidge.

'"Who's there?" will have to be a rhyme
We speak in verses all the time.'


'Oh right,' said Fidge, 'I see what you mean. I'll do a different sort of joke, then. I warn you, it's a bit feeble – my sister Minnie loves it, but she's only four. Here goes: What did one wall say to the other wall?'

The Wimblies looked at her blankly.

'Meet you at the corner!' supplied Fidge.

For a moment there was total silence, and then from behind the taxi rank came a series of familiar shrieks. The Yellows turned to look, and between them, Fidge glimpsed the open door of the Tourist Information Office. Inside, she could see two Orange Wimblies sitting behind a desk, leaning against each other, laughing hysterically.

'Right,' said Fidge. 'Can I go to the Mystic Grove now, please?'

The Yellow hurried over to one of the bikes and started to manouevre it out onto the road. Fidge was about to climb into the trailer when she hesitated; something had caught her eye just a moment ago, and she wanted another look. She walked over to the window of the tourist office and peered through the glass. Above the desk, where the Oranges were still hiccuping at her terrible joke, was a map of Wimbley Woo and a printed list of outings and excursions:

MORNING AT WIMBLEY FAIR
FOLLOWED BY AFTERNOON AT
# SWEET SHOP

MORNING AT WIMBLEY BOATING LAKE
FOLLOWED BY AFTERNOON AT
# SWEET SHOP

MORNING AT SWEET SHOP
FOLLOWED BY AFTERNOON AT
# SWEET SHOP

The entire list had been crossed out and the words **ALL EXCURSIONS CANCELLED** scrawled across it, but that wasn't what had caught her eye. It was the large framed picture that hung beside it, with OUR LEADER written on the frame. Above the words was a portrait. Fidge stared at it – at the tiny black eyes, the huge ears, the dark, dark red of the plush.

'But that's *Wed Wabbit!*' she said, incredulously.

There was a commotion behind her, and she turned to see Yellows running in all directions, panicking, yelping, bumping into each other, waving their hands in the air, heading for doorways and side-roads, dust puffing from under their feet. In seconds, the street was completely empty. Half a minute went by, and then one of the Yellows peered out from the shadows of a porch.

'Wed Wabbit,' repeated Fidge, experimentally.

The Yellow disappeared again.

'No, please don't go,' she called, quickly. 'Sorry, I won't say it again. Though I don't know what you're scared of, he's just a stupid toy.'

She waited for a while, but there was no answer, and no sign of any of the taxi drivers returning and with an inward groan, she entered the Tourist Information Office.

The Oranges straightened in their seats and nudged each other, looking at Fidge expectantly, like an audience waiting for a comedian to begin.

She took a deep breath. 'I have to get to the Mystic Grove,' she began, trying to speak in a calm, measured way so as not to set them off again, though the one on the left was already making a bursting noise. 'I need some directions, please, or a map. Like that one on the wall over there.'

The Orange on the right turned round to see where Fidge was pointing, leaned over a bit too far, fell off its chair, hit the floor with a rubbery thud and rolled across the room, screaming with laughter.

'I'll get it myself,' said Fidge. She climbed over the desk, squeezed between the honking, bleating Oranges, unpinned the map and took it outside. The street was still deserted.

The map was large and showed a web of white roads radiating across the green of the Wimbley landscape. There

73

was a sticker saying YOU ARE HERE beside an illustration of the Tourist Information Office, and not too far to the north-west was a dark green patch labelled MYSTIC GROVE, with a drawing of a Purple Wimbley poised beside it. There was a dirty mark on the Purple Wimbley's face and Fidge idly picked at it with a finger nail. It didn't come off.

'I'm just borrowing a taxi,' called Fidge, to the empty street. 'I'll try to bring it back, I promise. Unless someone would like to take me?'

There was no reply. She climbed onto the nearest bicycle, spread the map across the handlebars, and set off.

The first thing that occurred to her, as she pedalled along the lane, was that the Yellow Wimblies must be pretty fit. The trailer was heavy and awkward, pulling the bike off-course every time it went round a corner, and after a mile or so, she dismounted and had a look at the fittings to see whether she could detach the bike from the trailer. She couldn't manage it without a spanner, and she was about to resume cycling when the second thing occurred to her, a thought so weird that she heard herself gasp. She flattened out the map again, and peered closely at the tiny picture of the Purple Wimbley. The dirty mark on its face wasn't a dirty mark at all – it was a *moustache*. It looked exactly like the moustache that Minnie had drawn on every single Purple Wimbley in her copy of *The Land of Wimbley Woos*.

Fidge straightened up, frowning. She got back on the bike and set off again, but her thoughts were revolving faster than

74

her legs. *Fact*: she had just seen a portrait of Wed Wabbit. *Fact*: Wed Wabbit was not a character in the Wimbley Woo books. *Fact*: this wasn't just Wimbley Land, this was *Minnie's version* of Wimbley Land. *Fact:* when Fidge had thrown all Minnie's toys down the stairs at Graham's house, the thing that had happened next – the huge, soundless static explosion – must have somehow churned them together, and who knew what might—

'Taxi!'

Fidge braked and looked round. And was speechless.

'Room for a little one?' asked a fruity, fluting voice.

And as Fidge watched, unable to croak out a single syllable, a purple cloth elephant, the size of a carthorse, climbed into the trailer, smoothed down its pink skirt, batted its long pink eyelashes, tossed back its fluffy pink hair and smiled.

# THIRTEEN

'Breathe, darling,' said the elephant. 'You're not breathing.'

Fidge took a gulp of air. 'You're Eleanor Elephant,' she said.

'Oh, you recognize me!' The elephant looked delighted. 'Have we met professionally?'

'You're my sister's toy.'

'Life Coach,' corrected the elephant, using her trunk to extract a small card from a pocket in her skirt. 'Also available for Voice Development, Audition Technique and Confidence Workshops.' She flourished the card in front of Fidge; it showed the elephant in three different poses: looking wistfully into the distance, laughing wildly, and wearing glasses in front of a PowerPoint presentation. '"Eleanor Elephant" is my professional name though – all my friends call me Ella. Breathe, remember. In, then out.'

'What are you doing here?' asked Fidge, her voice a strangled squeak.

'You're speaking from the throat, darling. You need to speak from the lungs for a deeper, richer tone.'

Fidge took another gulp of air. 'What are you doing here?' she repeated, in a deeper, richer tone.

'*Doing* is such a frantic, breathless sort of word,' said Ella. 'At the moment I'm simply *being*. I'm absorbing and observing. When you find yourself unexpectedly in a new situation you need to be like a leaf in a stream, floating lightly on the current.'

'No you don't, you need to find out exactly what's going on. If I'd floated lightly on the current I'd have been arrested by a bunch of Blue Wimblies by now. They're everywhere and they're really strong and really nasty. And they seem to be working for Wed Wabbit, who belongs to my sister and I'm desperate to get him back to her and I also have to rescue a Pink who got into trouble because of me and I've *also* got to find the Mystic Grove because the Greys have asked me to sort everything out.'

The inside of Fidge's skull felt like a gridlocked traffic jam, full of bleeping, revving cars; her forehead was throbbing and she gave it a rub.

'Let's play catch!' said Ella, brightly.

'What?'

'You're very *tense*. So roll all of those tensions into a great big ball and throw it to me.' She stretched out her trunk invitingly.

'I've got to get going,' said Fidge. 'I've got stuff to do.'

'Try it, darling. You'll feel so much better. Roll up those tensions! Roll, roll, roll!'

Fidge made a half-hearted rolling gesture and then lobbed the invisible ball to Ella, who mimed catching something incredibly heavy.

'*Such* a huge weight, darling. And now do you feel better?'

Fidge was about to say no and then realized that she *did* feel a tiny bit better. She nodded, grudgingly. 'And now I really have to go. I've got to find the Purples.'

'Oh, a little trip to my absolute favourite colour,' said Ella, settling down in the trailer. 'How lovely!'

'But I don't know if I can move this thing with you in the back,' said Fidge.

Ella's smile faded, and she looked away and smoothed down her skirt. 'That was a little bit personal, darling,' she said, with quiet dignity. 'Size is something that I struggle with.'

'I just mean it's heavy anyway,' said Fidge, hastily. 'Even without a passenger. I'll give it a go.' She stood up on the pedals and managed, with a lot of effort, to get the taxi moving. The lane was on a slight downward slope, and they soon picked up speed, slaloming through a set of curves, crossing a hump-backed bridge with a crash that shook the axles and then rounding a corner to see a crossroads ahead.

'I'm a leaf!' called Ella. 'A leaf whirling through the rapids!'

'I think it's left here,' shouted Fidge over her shoulder, the map flapping unreadably in her grasp.

They hurtled into a narrow lane, overhung by trees, dipping through cool shadows before emerging suddenly into sunlight so strong that for a moment Fidge could barely see. And then her vision cleared and she could see only too well: a long, wide, straight road heading down into a valley, and at the bottom, a cluster of Blues standing behind a red-striped barrier.

'It's a roadblock,' she shouted, 'hold on tight!'

'See me twirl! See me spin! See me skip lightly over the twinkling currents!'

Fidge braced her arms against the handlebars and steered straight down the centre of the road. As the bike sped downhill, the map escaped from her grip and went flapping over the hedgerows and Fidge found herself yelling: a battle cry, fierce and loud. And ahead of her, the Blues were starting to realize what was coming towards them. There were five of them standing behind the roadblock. And then one of them dived behind the hedge and there were four. And then another three lost their nerve and ran to the side and finally there was only one Blue left, a megaphone held to its mouth.

'Our Leader made our orders clear
All strangers are to stop right—'

'Get out of the way, you idiot!' screamed Fidge.

With a *wumphhh* the taxi smashed straight through the barrier, sending chunks of wood cartwheeling through the air. As they thundered onwards, Fidge risked a glance over her shoulder and saw the Blue still upright, waving a megaphone that was now just a plastic handle.

'Darling, there's a crossroads coming up,' called Ella.

Fidge wrenched her attention back to the road. A signpost flashed by and then they were in another high-hedged lane, the bike slowing a little as the road began to rise, and suddenly there was a tight corner coming up and Fidge crammed on the brakes and hauled the handlebars round to the right and the taxi skidded in a complete circle, tyres screaming, before jolting to a halt with the front wheel jammed into a hedge.

She scrambled off the saddle and tried to pull the bike free. Twigs snapped and pinged; the trailer rocked.

'No offence, but you'll have to get out while I do this,' said Fidge, breathlessly.

'Just a moment, darling!' From her perch on the trailer, Ella was looking over the hedge. 'Did you say you were looking for the Mystic Grove?'

'Yes, but I've lost the map.'

'I can see it.'

'The map?'

'The Mystic Grove.'

'How do you know it's the Mystic Grove?'

'Because there's a sign over the entrance that says "Mystic Grove".'

'Oh, right.'

'And I can also see a stile a little further along this lane. Shall we investigate?'

Ella climbed out of the trailer, and Fidge followed her. The stile was just a few metres away, and through the wooden bars she could see a hay meadow, and beyond it a dense clump of trees with a faintly misty look to them. A path wound across the meadow towards the grove, and just above the place where it disappeared between the tree trunks, a purple sign swayed in the breeze.

'If I leave the taxi where it is,' said Fidge, 'the Blues might work out where we've gone.' She went back and pulled the bike free, and wheeled it around the next curve. Beyond, the lane swooped down a steep hill. Fidge positioned the taxi, gave it a shove and watched it dwindle to a rattling speck, and then she turned to follow Ella.

# FOURTEEN

It was odd but true, thought Fidge, as she walked through the field towards the Mystic Grove, that the presence of a six-foot-tall cloth elephant (in a skirt), walking just ahead of her was actually making her feel much better and more like her usual self. It was as if she'd glimpsed home. Ella was approximately ten times larger than she should have been, but apart from that, she was familiar in every detail: her fringe pinned back by Minnie's glittery hair slide, her skirt stained with a streak of Minnie's sticky cough medicine, her left ear creased and shrunken from Minnie's habit of chewing it when tired.

Ella swung round and caught Fidge staring. 'It's nothing serious – a work-related injury,' she said, tossing back the damaged ear. 'Now, darling, we're just about to meet some new people.'

'I know,' said Fidge.

'So can I just suggest a little facial relaxation?'

'What?'

'You're looking rather *stern*.'

'Oh.' Fidge tried a brief grin. 'How's that?'

'It's a *start*,' said Ella, tactfully. 'Now tell me about these Purples.'

'All I know is that Purple Wimblies *"understand the past and future of our Land"*. And I've been told to see them first.' She was struck by a thought. 'Do you know Wed Wabbit?'

'I've only been working with your sister since her last birthday, so probably not as well as you do. I do know that he and Minnie are very close.'

'He's her favourite toy, she takes him everywhere and she's always giving us his orders – "Wed Wabbit wants to stay up late, Wed Wabbit says to get more strawberry bubble bath, Wed Wabbit says he doesn't want to go to Auntie Claire's flute concert". He was the first thing Minnie asked for after the accident. She'll be missing him really, really badly.' The thought was painful; Fidge began to walk faster.

A delicate, silvery note floated across the meadow, followed by a second, and then a third, and from the shadows of the Grove, a trio of Purple Wimblies stepped into the sunlight.

Each carried a small gong; each wore a hooded purple

cloak; each had a scribbly black moustache. Together, in whispery, dreamy voices, they spoke:

'In and out and back and through
Follow strangers, follow do.
To the Mystic Woody Hollow
Follow follow follow follow.'

Softly, the Purple Wimblies tapped the gongs again, and then turned and melted into the darkness.

'Oh that was awfully good,' said Ella. 'Such a marvellous sense of drama.'

'Come on,' said Fidge, eagerly. 'Let's go!'

It felt as if they were entering a huge hall, the trunks of the trees like broad pillars holding up a roof of leaves. Through odd gaps in the canopy, sunlight sliced through to the forest floor, and ahead of Fidge and Ella, an edging of white stones marked the narrow path. The air smelled of spice and smoke, and there was the sound of distant chanting.

For the first time since arriving in Wimbley Woo, Fidge felt a stir of excitement. Soon, she'd be getting instructions; soon, instead of randomly wandering around she'd be able to make a proper plan and sort things out.

The path began to slope downwards, and the leaping light of a bonfire came into view. Around it danced a circle of Purple Wimblies, waving silver ribbons, leaping, swooping, dipping. More gongs sounded.

'Thrilling,' said Ella. 'The *hours* of rehearsal that must have gone into this . . .'

The chanting grew louder, until Fidge could make out the words:

'The long-awaited day is here
And soon we shall be freed from fear!
These strangers from another land,
Our prophecy will understand.'

She glanced at Ella. 'Prophecy? I thought they were just going to tell me what to do next.'

And then, abruptly, silence fell and the dancers paused, toes pointed, arms outstretched, silver ribbons drooping from their four-fingered hands.

A tall hooded Wimbley, holding a small log above its head, walked with slow dignity in front of the dancers and stood for a moment silhouetted against the fire. And then two Wimblies with flaming torches took their place on either side, and in the sudden light, Fidge saw that it wasn't a log that the central figure was holding, but a parchment scroll, tied with a purple ribbon. The figure spoke, its voice heavy with significance.

'When knotted anger rules the land
When holidays and sweets are banned
When rage soaks up the joy and fun
And colour out of everyone

We need to turn to four brave strangers
To release us from all dangers.'

Fidge glanced at Ella. '*Four* strangers?' she mouthed. 'But there's only two of us. And what's that stuff about knots and soaking up colour?'

The Wimbley spoke again.

'Come hither, strangers, break the seal.
The ancient secrets thus reveal
Just listen to the simple verse –
It's all you need to lift the curse.'

It held out the scroll to Fidge and she stepped forward, feeling as if she was accepting a prize at school.

'Thank you very much,' she said, awkwardly. Close up, the Purple's moustache looked freshly drawn, as if Minnie had just put away her felt-tip pen. Fidge swallowed. 'I'll open it, shall I?' she asked. The Purple nodded.

Fidge untied the ribbon and tugged at the wax seal. It broke into fragments, and the scroll sprang open to reveal a verse, written in spidery, elaborate handwriting.

'Would you like me to read it?' asked Ella, as Fidge squinted at the loops and curlicues. 'I have experience with scripts.'

'OK.'

Ella flung back her pink hair and lifted the scroll with her trunk. When she spoke, it was in a rolling, expressive voice that carried well beyond the circle of the fire.

'First seek the lost device and ring
The listener who knows everything
Then cast aside the words you use
For summing up the Wimbley Woos
And look again at every hue
A different word for each is true.
Then team new weaknesses and skills
To win the way to cure all ills.

And finally, just one of you
Must find the hardest thing to do
And when it's done – and only then –
You'll find your way back home again.'

There was a pause.

'Is that it?' asked Fidge.

Ella checked the other side of the scroll. 'Yes, that's all there is.'

The Purples had started chanting again:

'These strangers from another land
Our prophecy will understand,
It won't be hard for them to free
Our Wimbley Land from tyranny.'

'But . . .' Fidge peered over Ella's front leg and quickly re-read the verse on the scroll. 'I don't understand any of it. What Lost Device? What Ring? Who's the Listener? The whole middle bit's just vague rubbish and then it says we can't get back home till we've solved everything. How long's that going to take? I mean, Mum and Minnie are waiting for me *right now*!'

The Wimblies continued their infuriating chant:

'The simple clues they'll quickly crack
And soon we'll have our freedom back
So let us caper hand in hand
Because these strangers understand.'

'But I *don't* understand,' said Fidge, in frustration. 'Do you?' she asked, hopefully, swinging round to look at Ella.

'Darling, I'm still absorbing and observing. Interpretation comes last; first you must *feel* the role – it's only later that you can begin to *act*.'

The Wimblies were still singing:

'Hurray, hurray, hurray, hurray
These strangers here will save the day!
Like lightning they'll defeat the Blues
Because they understand the clues!'

'I've got to get out of here,' muttered Fidge; the singing, the darkness, the smoke, the frustration, seemed to wrap around her neck like a choking scarf, and she was longing for sunshine. She turned and began to head back.

'Thank you for everything!' she heard Ella calling to the Purples. 'Marvellous work. A five-star performance! The reviews will be *fabulous!*'

'Do you still have the scroll?' asked Fidge.

'Yes, darling. Safe and sound.'

Without the light of the bonfire to aim for, it was hard to pick out the path, and Fidge found herself stumbling over roots, and being smacked in the face by leafy branches, while behind her, Ella smashed through the undergrowth. By the time they emerged from the Grove, it was clear that they had gone badly wrong. Instead of a grassy meadow, there was a ploughed field ahead of them, and a brisk stream bordered by an avenue of tall trees. And instead of bright sunshine, the view was steeped in the blueish light of early evening. Fidge realized suddenly how tired she was, and how thirsty. She knelt beside the stream and scooped up mouthfuls of water, and then splashed some over her face.

'It tastes OK,' she said to Ella.

There was no reply. The cloth elephant had walked a little way along the avenue, her head tilted thoughtfully, her ears extended like wing flaps.

'What's up?' asked Fidge, joining her.

'Listen, darling,' said Ella. 'Can you hear what I'm hearing?'

Fidge listened, and gasped.

Someone was calling her name.

# FIFTEEN

'Fidge!' shouted Graham, from halfway up the tree. *'FIDGE!'*

She was standing directly below him, and he saw her snap her head back and gape upwards.

'Graham!' she said, in astonishment.

'You have to help me. I've been stuck up here for hours and hours. It's lucky I haven't fainted.'

'Are you injured, or something?'

'No.'

'Why don't you just climb down then?'

'What?'

'*Climb down*. It should be easy. There are loads of branches,

90

it's practically like a stepladder. There's even a big platform just above you.'

'I know. I was on it.'

'Why?'

'I got kidnapped by a group of abseiling dustbins.'

'What colour dustbins?'

'Green.'

'Green are daring,' shouted Fidge.

'What are you talking about? Why's there a purple elephant standing next to you?'

'Just climb down, Graham.'

'I can't, all right? I got this far, but I can't get any further. Climbing's the sort of thing that you find easy, but I have more important skills. And if you don't help me it'll be your fault if I fall and *die*. The way that Dr Carrot did.'

'I am not dead,' said a firm, level voice from the stream. 'The willow broke my fall. I have merely chosen not to communicate for a while.'

'Who's Dr Carrot?' asked Fidge. She walked over to the bank, where a weeping willow hung over the water, and pushed her way through the drooping branches. The top half of an enormous plastic carrot was sticking out of the stream.

'Good afternoon,' it said, from a mouth that was a single black line.

'You're Graham's trans-thingy object!'

'*Transitional*,' corrected Graham from the tree, but Fidge

was scarcely listening. An idea had leaped into her mind and she was mentally ticking off the list of all the things she'd thrown down into Graham's basement: Wed Wabbit, the pop-up Wimbley book, Ella Elephant, the plastic carrot – and there was one other item, a toy about which she'd completely forgotten . . .

'I know what it means!' she shouted.

'What, darling?' Ella poked her head into the leafy cave.

'The Purple prophecy, I think I know what the first bit of the instructions means – can you read it again?'

Ella took the scroll out of her skirt pocket and unfurled it.

'First seek the lost device and ring,
The listener who knows everything.'

she intoned. Fidge punched the air in triumph. 'The "lost device" is Minnie's mobile phone! She's got a toy one covered in fake diamonds and it's obviously in Wimbley Land somewhere, just like everything else I chucked down those stairs, and we've got to find it and then *ring* someone.'

She could hear Graham shouting.

'Hang on!' she called.

'You see what happens,' said Ella, 'when you allow yourself to *relax* into an experience? Interpretations simply *flood* in.'

There was the sound of a throat being cleared. 'Reluctant as I am to interrupt,' said the carrot, 'I've now been relaxed into this particular flood for nearly three hours and I would be grateful for some assistance.'

'Oh right, sorry,' said Fidge. It seemed odd to apologize to a vegetable, but this one had an air of crisp authority and she hurried over to help. Graham was still shouting.

'I said hang *on*!' she called to him again. It was difficult to get a grip on Dr Carrot, and it seemed somehow rude to haul on the green plastic sprout on the top of her head.

'If only I could help,' said Ella, 'but I have a little bit of a back problem, ever since attending a circus skills course. I shouldn't have tried the trapeze.'

'Loos!' Graham seemed to be yelling.

Fidge was lying on the bank, groping under the water. 'You'll just have to go in the woods, like I did,' she called.

'*Blues*, you idiot, I said *Blues*! Everywhere! Hundreds of them!'

And before Fidge could get up, or even turn round, the curtain of drooping branches was thrust aside and the space beneath the willow was invaded by a unit of red-sashed Blue Wimblies, who dragged Ella away, and hauled the carrot from the water. They tied Fidge's arms behind her back and jerked her out into the open, and though she twisted and fought against the cold blue hands, she couldn't break free. Graham was still screaming, but now it was because he was being lowered on a rope from the tree, upside down. As he neared the ground, he locked eyes with Fidge.

'This is all your fault,' he said, hysterically. 'You wouldn't listen to me.' And then he was flung over the shoulder of one of the Blues, and carried off, drumming his feet against the cylindrical body.

Fidge struggled. 'We've done nothing wrong!' she yelled at the one with the red beret. Its face, close-up, was horrible: painted eyes that narrowed sternly, a dark slit of a mouth that widened into a shout:

'Our Leader's wish is very clear
We do not welcome strangers here
Our Leader has a place for those
Who break his rules or dare oppose.'

And then it nodded at her captor, and Fidge was given a shove between the shoulder blades that sent her stumbling into the twilight.

# SIXTEEN

The bicycle truck hurtled through the darkness, six Yellows pedalling, their legs a pale blur. Locked in the back, hands tied, Graham, Fidge and Ella were flung from side to side as the truck veered round one corner after another.

'That *hurt*,' shouted Graham, as a purple trunk smacked him on the ear.

'Sorry, darling. Accident.'

Dr Carrot lay on the floor; the Blues, apparently confused by the fact that she didn't have any arms, had handcuffed her wheels together, with the result that she'd fallen over on the first corner.

'I would be very much obliged,' she said, 'if everyone could avoid actually standing on my *face*.'

Through the window, Fidge glimpsed a full moon rising above the hedgerows.

'Where are they taking us?' wailed Graham.

'I think I know,' said Fidge. The road was beginning to rise, and silhouetted against the white disc of the moon, she could see a hill, and on top of it the unmistakable outline of a castle, decked with flags.

The truck swayed round another couple of corners and then jerked to a halt, throwing everyone to the floor.

'Ow,' said Dr Carrot, pointedly.

Fidge was still clambering to her feet when the guards unlocked the back door and hauled her, with the others, out onto the road. In the cold blue moonlight, she could see a stretch of water spanned by a heavily guarded wooden drawbridge. On the far side, a path led steeply up towards a monstrous gate in the castle wall. Red Beret shouted to his troops:

'Come now! Our Leader mustn't wait.
Rewards are cancelled when we're late.'

They set off at a fast pace, a guard at each shoulder, Dr Carrot's wheels rumbling over the bridge across the moat and then squeaking as she started uphill.

'I'm scared,' said Graham, breathlessly. 'I'mscaredI'm scaredI'mscared—'

'Don't be,' said Fidge. She glanced sideways at her captors and then lowered her voice to a mutter. 'The thing is, this leader they keep going on about is just an ugly old stuffed toy.' And then she thought of the last time she'd seen Wed Wabbit, lying tied in a knot on the cellar steps, one eye staring furiously up at her, and she felt a wave of unease.

The hill steepened. Behind her, she could hear Ella panting.

'Would you mind awfully, darlings, if we slowed down just a tiny bit? I've not been able to get to the gym for a while – terribly, *terribly* busy at work.'

Ahead of them, the huge gate swung open, and they were marched through into a courtyard, its walls hung with flaming torches. Shadows leaped and shrank across the stones.

'Gorgeous lighting,' said Ella, breathing heavily. '*Super-dramatic.*'

'Silence!' shouted a guard. 'In just one minute
This room will have Our Leader in it.'

The gate crashed shut behind them and Graham gave a whine of fear. Fidge glanced quickly around, searching for possible escape routes, and saw three doorways in the opposite wall of the courtyard. The nearest to her had the word REWARDS written above the lintel, and was guarded by a pair of Blues; the second was labelled PUNISHMENTS and was fastened with a series of heavy bolts, while the third was deep-set into a gloomy archway.

She looked again at the REWARDS door; the two Blues

standing guard were much heavier than the others with large, baggy stomachs, and both of them were chewing, their expressions serene.

'I wonder if . . .' she started to say, and then stopped; she could hear a low rumbling noise and the ground beneath her began to vibrate.

'Earth tremor!' shouted Graham.

'No,' said Fidge, pointing, 'look!'

The wall at one end of the courtyard seemed to be splitting in two, a dark crack widening at the centre of it. Two words written in golden letters glittered in the torchlight as they moved slowly apart:

THRONE          ROOM

'It's not a wall, it's a giant set of doors,' said Fidge.

A troop of Blues marched out of the dark gap and formed two parallel lines, like a broad corridor. Between them, something large began to move slowly and smoothly out of the shadows.

Fidge's mouth dropped open.

She could see wheels, huge pink wheels with flowers on the hub. Above the wheels was a metal framework, decorated with stickers of dancing kittens.

'Minnie's toy buggy,' she said, her lips hardly moving, her gaze sliding upward to its occupant.

She'd expected Wed Wabbit to be big – after all, Ella

Elephant and Dr Carrot were as large as full-grown adults. She'd even expected Wed Wabbit to be *ridiculously* big – as large as a polar bear, maybe, or even a hippo. She hadn't expected him to be *twenty feet tall*, lolling in a gigantic buggy, pushed by a team of panting, straining Yellows. And she hadn't expected him still to be tied in a knot, though one of his ears had worked loose, and was sticking up at an odd angle. His expression was one of fury.

'Knotted anger!' whispered Ella. 'Do you remember what the Purple said? *When knotted anger rules the land, When holidays and sweets are banned, When rage soaks up the joy and fun and colour out of everyone . . .'*

The buggy came to a halt in the centre of the courtyard, and the Yellows scurried away again into the darkness.

For a moment there was silence, and then Wed Wabbit spoke – not in the roar that might have matched his size, but in a hideous eardrum-shredding squeak, like the noise of someone dragging their finger down a giant party balloon.

'BWING THE PWISONERS FORWARD.'

Fidge and the others were grabbed by the Blues and thrust into a row immediately between the buggy wheels. Looking up, they could only see the huge red velvet mound of Wed Wabbit's stomach, and part of one of his feet.

'NO, NO NO, USE YOUR BWAINS, GUARDS!

MOVE THE PWISONERS BACK TO WHERE
I CAN SEE THEM! HUWWY UP OR THERE
WILL BE NO WEWARDS TONIGHT!'

There was a whirl of panicking guards, and Fidge and the others were grabbed once again and dragged back a few steps. Now they could see Wed Wabbit staring crookedly down at them, legs entangled, one ear still folded over his face. His eyes were like liquorice discs, blank and sinister; his mouth was stitched in harsh black thread.

His head swivelled slowly as he looked from Ella, to Fidge to Graham to—

'Good evening,' said Dr Carrot.

'SILENCE!!!' screamed Wed Wabbit, and the shrill, splintered sound was almost unbearable.

Graham rammed his hands over his ears.

'Speaking as a voice professional,' said Ella, nervously but clearly, 'you're going to do the most frightful damage to your vocal chords, screeching like that.'

'I SAID WEMAIN SILENT!! THOSE WHO
BWEAK MY WULES WILL FACE MY WAGE!!!'

'What's he *talking* about?' muttered Graham, through clenched teeth. 'I don't understand. What wage?'

'He means "rage". He can't say the letter "r",' said Fidge, under her breath. 'Just like Minnie.'

'So why does he keep choosing words that begin with that letter then? It sounds ridiculous.'

## 'STOP WHISPEWING!! MY WOYAL WULE IS THAT NO ONE SHOULD AWWIVE IN MY COUNTWY WITHOUT INVITATION AND YOU STWANGERS HAVE TWANSPAWENTLY BWOKEN THIS WULE!!!'

'Try and speak from the *chest* rather than the *neck*,' suggested Ella, helpfully.

Wed Wabbit began to quiver, like a kettle about to boil.

## 'SILENCE!!! I WEPEAT, SILENCE!!!!'

His voice was twice as loud as before, twice as fast and wobbling with emotion, and as he spoke, he visibly swelled.

## 'MY WIGID WEQUIREMENT IS THAT MY WOYAL WEQUESTS ARE MET WITH A WAPID WESPONSE!!!

# AND WEMEMBER, WHEN I SAY "WAPID", I MEAN WEALLY, *WEALLY* WAPID!!!'

His folded ear pinged suddenly upward, freed from the knot.

There was a long pause, followed by a tiny muffled squeak from Graham, as if he was trying not to cry.

Fidge glanced at him, and then just as quickly looked away again, but it was too late. She knew instantly, from his strained, pink face that it wasn't tears he was holding back, it was *laughter*, and though it was the worst possible time and the worst possible place to be feeling such a thing, she was immediately overcome by the same urge. She looked down, biting the insides of her cheeks, clenching her fists, trying to remind herself of the appalling seriousness of their situation, but she could feel a great ball of hysteria forming in her chest, trying to force its way up into her mouth.

# 'WIMBLEY LAND HAS BEEN WUN IN A WEGWETTABLE WAY, BUT NOW THE TIME OF WECKONING HAS

COME, WEQUIWING
A BWEAK FROM THE
PAST AND A CWACK
DOWN ON TWEATS AND
WELAXATION. IT WILL
TAKE AN EXTWEMELY
STWONG STWUGGLE TO
WIGHT THESE WONGS
AND I—'

Graham let out a huge snort, and Fidge found she couldn't hold back any longer and they were suddenly both yelping with helpless, uncontrollable laughter – Graham doubled up, Fidge with tears actually running down her cheeks. Through the blurred view, she could see the Blues staring at her with shocked expressions.

# 'WESTWAIN THEM!'

screamed Wed Wabbit, and he grew even larger, so that the buggy strained and buckled beneath him.

# 'WESTLE THEM TO THE DUNGEONS AND TOMOWWOW THEY WILL FACE THE TEWWIBLE WEALITY OF THE PUNISHMENTS WOOM!!!'

And though the words were a threat, and the future chilling, Fidge felt too weak to do anything but shake her head and giggle feebly, as a Blue guard grabbed her by the shoulders and marched her towards the third door in the wall.

# SEVENTEEN

**B**eyond the door was a spiral staircase leading downwards; the light was dim and there was little to hold on to. As each corkscrew turn took her deeper and deeper beneath the castle, Fidge felt the laughter die in her throat. Ahead she could see Dr Carrot being carried by one of the guards while behind her, Ella kept exclaiming over the steepness of the steps. Graham was at the back somewhere and she wondered whether he was still finding it funny; she suspected not.

'Where to now?' asked Ella, cheerfully, when they reached the bottom, but there was no need for a reply; a single dank passageway stretched ahead, and at the end of it was a circular room, lined with cell doors and lit by a solitary bulb. The only furniture in the room was a stone drinking fountain, right in the middle.

Fidge looked quickly around and saw that she'd been right about Graham: his face was pale, his expression desperate. Dr Carrot, meanwhile, had her eyes shut and even Ella seemed subdued.

The Blue with the red beret took a key from its belt and wagged it sternly at them.

'Your prison sentence starts today
This dreadful dungeon's where you'll stay
Until the morning, when it's time
To start repayment for your crime.'

'But we haven't done anything wrong,' said Fidge. 'We didn't *ask* to turn up here – all I want to do is get home!'

There was no answer, and the next moment she was bundled towards one of the cell doors. As it opened, she felt her hands being untied and before she could turn or duck or run, she was given a push that sent her stumbling into the cell. She tried to stop herself, but tripped and fell full-length onto a prickly surface. Behind her, the door slammed shut and the key twisted in the lock.

She rolled over. For a moment the only noise was her own ragged breathing. She was lying on what felt like a bristly doormat. Most of the cell was in darkness, but directly above her a familiar pattern of lights fluttered across the ceiling – pale pink silhouettes of moons and stars and cats. It looked just like the night light that Minnie had been given last Christmas, and which she'd claimed to hate because it gave her bad dreams.

What was a night light doing in a dungeon? Fidge was groping for an answer when she heard Graham scream – an urgent, terrified scream – and she scrambled to her feet and plunged through the darkness to the door and pressed her mouth to the keyhole, the planking rough against her nose.

'What's the matter?' she called, but there was no reply. Putting her eye to the hole, she could see a section of flagstoned floor. Nothing else was visible.

She straightened up, and ran her hands across the door. There was a square hole at the centre, spanned by a row of bars. Through the spaces between them she could touch a sheet of wood – a shutter, perhaps. She tugged at the bars but the door didn't move in the slightest, and kicking it simply hurt her foot.

'Are you all right?' she shouted. 'Graham?'

She remembered how they'd both laughed at Wed Wabbit – the first time that they'd ever been in agreement about *anything* – and she gave the bars a last, frustrated, tug before giving up. There was clearly no way of getting out before the morning. The thought of Mum and Minnie still waiting for her at the hospital – waiting, worrying, wondering where she was – was just unbearable, and she shoved the thought away, and began to explore the cell one step at a time, trailing her fingertips along the wall. She felt a ledge, and on it an empty cup, a very squashy banana, and a chained metal jug filled with water. She poured a cupful and began to drink, spluttering violently as she realized that it wasn't water but milk – warm milk, with a slight skin on top.

Good thing Minnie's not here, she thought, wiping her mouth; her sister always made a huge fuss about drinking warm milk, it was one of the things she really hated.

'*Oh!*' said Fidge, out loud, remembering a few other things that Minnie really hated: scary night lights, and overripe bananas, and bristly doormats that hurt your feet '*Oh*. I get it.'

This wasn't any old loathsome dungeon, this was *Minnie's* idea of a loathsome dungeon, which meant that somewhere in the darkness there might also be yoghurt with bits in, and possibly a daddy-long-legs or two.

She took a gulp of milk. It was funny how, when you really missed someone, you even missed the annoying things about them. She set the cup down and then gasped. She could hear something – *someone* – in the cell with her. She could hear them breathing.

'Hello,' she said, her mouth instantly dry again.

The breathing continued. It seemed to be coming from the back of the cell. Low down. Snuffly. Regular.

'Who's there?' asked Fidge, and she could hear her voice trembling. It was one thing to be able to climb and run and pedal her way out of danger, but to be trapped in darkness with something unknown was truly horrible. Perhaps the same thing had just happened to Graham; perhaps that was why he'd screamed.

'Answer me,' she said, trying to sound commanding. 'Just say who you are.'

There was a hitch in the rhythm of the breathing and a rustle of straw as Whoever-it-was moved around slightly, muttered, 'Nyum nyum nyum nyum nyum,' and then yawned. The snorty, regular breathing began again. Fidge relaxed very slightly; Whoever-it-was was deeply, deeply asleep.

She edged over to the cell door, and sat down with her back against the wood. She suddenly felt appallingly tired – her muscles as slack as spaghetti, her brain like an over-stuffed pillow. What she wanted, more than anything else, was to lie down and go to sleep, but how could she do that when she was sharing a cell with someone unknown and potentially dangerous?

It was vital that she stayed alert.

Vital.

Absolutely *vital*.

# EIGHTEEN

She was woken by a crash directly above her head and she jerked forward into a crouch, heart galloping. Light spilled into the cell – someone had slid open the shutter in the door, and a blue hand was poking a tin tray through a slot at the bottom of the bars.

Cautiously, she reached up and took it, and the hand disappeared again. The tray was strewn with wholemeal toast crusts, the sort that Minnie would never eat. There was also yoghurt with bits in, a bowl of dull-looking muesli – all oats and seeds – and some slices of apple that had obviously been left for a while and had gone brown. Despite the unappetizing look of it all, Fidge's stomach rumbled, and she'd just started to eat when there was a yawn from the back of the cell.

'Who's that?' she demanded, scrambling to her feet, crust in hand. Hunger had briefly made her forget that she wasn't alone, but now the other occupant emerged from the shadows and she was oddly relieved to see that it was only a Wimbley, a Wimbley with a hat – no, a Wimbley with a *crown*. It approached, yawning, and gazed down at the tray.

'Would you mind awfully if I ate
The muesli?' it asked. 'Biddly bate,' it added, half-heartedly.

'No, go ahead – take it,' said Fidge. 'Are you the king of Wimbley Woo?'

'Yes, hello, lovely meeting you
It's splendid all the *mph mph mph*,' replied the king, taking
      a mouthful of muesli halfway through the second line.

'But . . .' Fidge peered at him. The light coming through the bars wasn't very bright, but it was strong enough for her to see something that made her frown. 'On your statue there was a verse that said you were every colour and every hue. Shouldn't you look like a rainbow?'

The king shook his head.

'If you mix every single hue
You'll end up with my colour. True.'

Fidge nodded slowly. She was thinking of Minnie's box of plasticine, which had once been a spectrum of brilliance but which now contained a single sludge-coloured ball faintly streaked with colour. If the ball had been rolled into a cylinder and given arms and legs, it would have looked just like the King.

'So what can you tell me about this place?' she asked. 'How did you end up in prison? How did Wed Wabbit take over? Who else is here? How's it guarded? Have you tried escaping?'

The king wiped his mouth and looked at her absently.

'Sorry, I didn't hear your question.
This muesli's rather good. Bim bestion.'

'*Bim bestion?*' repeated Fidge. 'What's that mean?'
The king sighed.

'It's awfully dreary every time
To have to finish with a rhyme.'

'You managed it that time,' said Fidge.

'Yes, but it's a crashing bore,
Makes conversation such a chore.
Instead of pleasant, idle banter
One's forced to end with words like' – he rolled his eyes
– "*canter*".

Which haven't got the slightest bearing
On the topic that we're airing.
It's easier just to speak as normal
And add odd syllables. Bim Bormal.'

Fidge nodded, but she was only half-listening, distracted by the sound of a raised voice. Standing on tiptoe, she peered out between the bars at the circular room. Four other cell doors were visible from her viewpoint and a tray was being shoved back between the bars of the nearest one. It crashed to the floor, scattering crusts in all directions.

'If they're not made with organic flour, I'm not eating them!' shouted a voice from the cell.

'Graham!' called Fidge.

Her cousin's pale face appeared between the bars. 'I need help,' he shouted. 'I'm sharing a cell with a hideous pink barrel that keeps asking for hugs.'

'I bet that's the Wimbley I saw being arrested,' said Fidge. 'It won't hurt you.'

'How do you know?'

'Because Pinks are harmless.'

'Who says?'

'*I* do. I know loads and loads about Wimbley Woos. In fact, the only person who knows more about Wimbley Land than me is Minnie. She knows *everything*.' There was something strangely familiar about that last sentence and she was just trying to work out what it was, when she heard a trilling voice.

'Fidgie, darling!'

The tip of a purple trunk was waving frantically between the bars of another cell, and Fidge felt a surge of relief.

'Hello, Ella,' she shouted back. 'Are you with Dr Carrot?'

'No, she's in the next cell. I'm sharing with the Oldest and Wisest of the Grey Wimblies, who apparently used to be the king's chief adviser.' Ella didn't sound quite as bouncy as usual.

'That might be helpful,' called Fidge. 'Greys are wise and rarely wrong.'

'Yes, darling, it's been telling me in considerable detail for several *hours* now, how very, very wise and almost never wrong they are.'

Behind Fidge, the king groaned.

'They're awfully dull, those wise old Greys,' he remarked.
'They won't shut up for days and days
They never chat, they just inform
In endless detail. Diddly—'

'Dorm,' supplied Fidge. 'But did you learn anything useful?' she called to Ella. 'Like, what's in the Punishments Room that Wed Wabbit was talking about?'

But as she spoke, she could hear the thunder of approaching feet, and the shouting of guards.

'I think,' said Ella, quietly, 'that we're just about to find out.'

# NINETEEN

Fidge stood in front of the door labelled PUNISHMENTS, her arms gripped by a pair of guards, her throat tight, her breath short.

A guard with a red beret stepped forward and tugged at the first bolt. It slid open with a noise like a whip crack.

'I believe that it is customary to hold a trial before punishment is decided upon,' said Dr Carrot.

Red Beret ignored this. The second bolt shot back.

'I'm going to faint,' said Graham. 'Any second now. I can feel myself going.'

'I think we should work on our inner spirit animals,' suggested Ella. 'Let's imagine we're eagles, soaring high, high above the valley of fear.'

The door began to swing open. Fidge took a gulp of air, bracing herself for what she might see – and then let it out again with a puzzled grunt.

She was looking at a large white-walled room containing six extremely long plastic-topped dining tables, each large enough for at least fifty people. On the floor at one end of the room was a pile of cleaning materials.

Red Beret turned to the prisoners, his expression stern.

'You have one hour to wipe these clean,' he said, harshly.
'These table tops must be pristine.
So start at once and don't delay
And use the gloves, sponge, cloth and spray.'

'What?' asked Fidge, stupidly. Her hands were suddenly released and she was pushed into the room with the other prisoners. The door slammed shut behind them.

'And don't forget the sticky rings,' shouted Red Beret,
    through the panelling.
'Make sure you use those scourer things.
If it's not clean when I return,
A second punishment you'll earn.'

For a moment, they all stood and looked at each other: Fidge, Ella, the Oldest and Wisest of the Greys, Dr Carrot, the King, the Pink and Graham. And then the Pink spoke.

'I'm sure we all feel in a muddle.
Would anybody like a cud—'

'*No*,' said Graham sharply.

'Well, I certainly would,' said Ella, galloping across the room towards the Pink. It looked slightly startled as she squashed it into a vast embrace.

Graham stood with his arms folded, staring at the tables. 'What on earth's all this?' he asked.

'I think I know,' said Fidge. 'This would be Minnie's idea of a horrible punishment. It's her job at home, you see – to wipe down the table after meals – and it always takes her ages. The only thing she hates more than having to tidy up is being made to sit still.' She walked over to the nearest table and grimaced at the covering of smears, crumbs, grease stains and juice spills. 'We'd better get on with it, I suppose. At least we can talk while we're doing it and try and make some sort of plan.'

'I can't do anything at the moment,' said Graham, flopping down in a corner. 'I'm too tired. I'll be ill if I don't have a sleep.'

'Yes, I too feel a touch exhausted,' said the king.
'I'll rest a while, then help. Rex Rorsted.'

'Oh, thanks a bunch,' said Fidge.
'Well, *I'll* help, darling,' said Ella, 'and so shall my new

friend the Pink, and I'm sure Dr Carrot will too.' She turned to the carrot. 'Could we possibly hang a bucket around your stem? And maybe place another one on your little platform? I'm not able to carry anything heavy, you see, since my back injury.'

'Delighted to be of service,' said Dr Carrot, shooting a disapproving glance at Graham.

'And what about you?' Fidge asked the Oldest and Wisest, who was standing doing absolutely nothing. It gave a little start of amazement, its eyes widening.

'I'd love to be of help to you.
But I'm a Grey. We *Think* not *Do*.'

'What about trying both at the same time?' she said, but the Grey just stared back at her, apparently shocked by the suggestion. Fidge shook her head, and turned away. There was a lot of work to be done.

'You know the start of the instructions in the prophecy?' she said to Ella, as they scrubbed and sluiced.

'First seek the lost device and ring,
The listener who knows everything?'

'Yes. Well, the lost device is Minnie's phone – I'd already worked that out – but I've just realized who the "listener who knows everything" is.'

'Who, darling?'

'It's Minnie! Minnie knows every single thing there is to know about Wed Wabbit and the Wimbley Woos, so she's the one we have to ask advice from. So we've got to somehow get out of this castle and then find the phone and speak to Minnie . . .' She stopped, a lump in her throat at the thought of hearing her sister's voice. 'Speak to Minnie and ask her what to do.' She scrubbed hard at a sticky mark on the table and remembered the wide view of Wimbley Land that she'd seen from the top of the monument. Near the horizon had been an odd cluster of pink, twinkling lights . . .

'Hi,' said a voice behind Fidge.

She turned to see Graham.

'I thought you were having a rest.'

'I tried to sleep, but . . .' He glanced over his shoulder and lowered his voice. 'That Grey Wimbley is unbelievably boring. It kept droning on and on and I couldn't stand it any longer.'

'Well, grab a sponge then.'

'What?'

'Grab a sponge. Start cleaning.' She nodded her head towards a bucket.

Graham stared at her. 'You want me to wipe the tables?'

'Yes.'

'But I don't know how to.'

Fidge nearly groaned in disbelief. She nearly shouted, *'How useless* are *you?'* But something had changed about Graham's manner – there was a hesitancy that hadn't been there before – and instead, she picked up the bucket and held it out to him. 'Why don't you just have a go?' she said.

Slowly, cautiously, Graham reached into it, his expression that of someone about to pull a dead frog out of a pond.

'Good,' said Dr Carrot, approvingly, 'and now squeeze out the sponge. That's it, that's the way. And now take it over to the table.'

They all watched as Graham began to dab feebly at the stains.

'Try to use long wiping movements,' added Ella. 'Perhaps a little bit more pressure?'

'Stop staring at me,' said Graham through gritted teeth. 'Just carry on talking.'

Fidge nodded. 'OK. Well, if we're planning to escape, the first thing to tackle is how to get out of the actual cells. Does anyone have any ideas?'

The Pink raised a hand.

'Is your idea to do with hugging?' asked Fidge.

The Pink nodded.

'Right,' said Fidge. 'We'll bear it in mind. Anyone else?'

'Can someone just break the doors down?' suggested Graham. 'Someone who's really big and heavy?'

There was a long pause during which everyone did a lot of cleaning and no one looked at Ella.

'OK,' said Fidge, 'any more ideas?'

'I noticed,' said Dr Carrot, 'that the guard with the red beret keeps the cell key on his belt, on a hook – it's the same key for every door. I wonder if it might be possible for someone with arms to reach through the bars and snatch it. If we wait until we're locked in for the night, it might not be noticed until the morning.'

'It would have to be someone with very long, thin arms,' said Fidge.

'Or someone, darlings . . .' said Ella, straightening up and tossing her hair back, 'who has a *trunk*!'

Fidge was about to say *Brilliant!* when she heard the sound of bolts being drawn back. 'Quickly, quickly,' she called, 'we've only cleaned four and a half tables out of the six!'

But the door was already opening.

They'd run out of time.

# TWENTY

The day wore on.

The second punishment consisted of being forced to sit still, without fidgeting, on a row of hard chairs, while listening to a recording of a ninety minute flute concert. They failed the task when Ella fell asleep and slumped heavily onto Fidge, creating a domino effect all along the row, ending with the Pink being knocked off its chair.

Then, while the prisoners ate their lunch (broccoli soup), a team of Blues set up the third punishment, bringing into the room a chest of drawers, a small desk and a bedroom door, all of which were covered with extremely gluey stickers of ponies, rainbows and puppies. The half-hour they were given to peel all the stickers off again was nowhere near long enough, especially as the only person with any fingernails was Fidge (Graham's were bitten).

The final task was the worst. Red Beret gave them each a dustpan and brush and then opened a huge packet of silver glitter and threw it all over the room. Even the King roused himself to help with this one, but by the end of ninety minutes the prisoners looked like a bunch of Christmas decorations, and the floor was almost as sparkly as when they'd started.

'Tomorrow we'll begin anew
With harder, longer tasks for you,' announced Red Beret.
'Each one you fail will add a day
On to the length of time you'll stay.'

'We have to escape *tonight*,' muttered Graham, out of the side of his mouth, as they were marched back to their cells.

Fidge nodded, still brushing specks of glitter from her sleeves. 'When they collect the dinner trays,' she whispered. 'That's when I'll give the signal to do what we agreed.'

Graham gave her the thumbs up, and it was so odd seeing him do something so normal and ordinary, that she almost managed to smile in reply.

Back in Fidge's cell, the king slumped down with a sigh and closed his eyes.

'Could I just ask you not to wake me
When they bring the supper? Bakebee.'

Fidge stared at him. 'But that's when we're going to create a distraction to allow Ella to steal the key. We worked out the plan when we were sweeping up the glitter – you were there, weren't you listening?'

The king shook his head.

'I see you're keen to get away,' he said, placidly.
'But, frankly, I'd prefer to stay.'

'But you're supposed to be in charge of Wimbley Land! Aren't you worried about what Wed Wabbit's done to your country? Don't you want to get out there and change it?'

The king took off his crown and gave it a rueful look.

'It's really not my sort of thing.
I never asked to be a king.
I'm not at all the active sort
I'd rather just relax. Dip dort.'

He gave the five-pointed crown a quick polish, jammed it back on his head, folded his hands and went to sleep.

'Useless,' muttered Fidge. She could hear footsteps approaching; seconds later, the cell shutter slid back and a tray was shoved in through the slot. On the menu tonight was a blue cheese and coriander bake followed by rice pudding with no jam; Fidge choked down a few mouthfuls, and waited impatiently for the guards to come back to collect the trays.

Red Beret was with them, supervising, the key dangling from a hook on its belt. Quickly, Fidge propped her tin tray at an angle against the wall and then stamped on it. She picked up the badly bent result and shoved it through the slot beneath the bars. It wedged halfway.

'Oh no!' she shouted. 'My tray's got stuck!'

A grumpy-looking guard walked across, and started pulling at the tray. In the background Fidge could see Red Beret standing watching, hands on hips. Behind him, Ella's trunk snaked out between the bars of her cell, but the key was just too far away for her to reach.

Fidge banged the tray with her fork, as a signal to the next distracter.

'Excuse me.' Dr Carrot's voice floated out from the cell at the end. 'Could I speak to the Wimbley in charge, please?'

Red Beret turned, irritably.

'I am not in any way satisfied with the conditions in which we are being held,' continued Dr Carrot. 'I would like to know if you have an official complaints procedure.'

Ella's trunk made another grope for the key, and was just about to snatch it when the guard outside Fidge's cell gave a fierce jerk to the stuck tray, freeing it so suddenly that it spun across the room like a Frisbee and hit Red Beret on the back of the head.

'You clumsy fool,' it bellowed, striding towards the guard.

'I'll see that you
Don't get the sweets that you've been due.
And don't protest with, "If" or "But"
Your time in the Reward Room's *cut.*'


The Blue guard sagged pitifully at the knees, looking as if it was about to burst into tears and Fidge felt like doing the same thing, because Red Beret was moving away from the cells now, ordering the guards to close the shutters and preparing to leave for the night. The chance of getting the key was slipping away. She had to think quickly.

What would stop a Blue in its tracks?

'Hey!' she shouted, through the bars. 'Who wants some sweets?'

The effect of her words was immediate. The guards swivelled round, mouths open.

'I've got white chocolate buttons,' she called. The guards edged closer, their eyes huge and eager. 'I've got lemon sherbets, licorice laces and . . . and . . .'

'Jelly beans!' yelled Graham from the next cell. 'Fudge in six different flavours. Caramels. Peanut brittle.'

'And for those of you with more sophisticated palates,' called Dr Carrot, 'I have a selection of fine pralines coated in Belgian chocolate.'

The guards were clustering around the doors now, peering eagerly through the bars, ignoring the furious shouts of Red Beret who was hurrying from one group to another, trying to close the shutters and drag the Wimblies away. Fidge caught a glimpse of a waving purple trunk, and then the shutter on her own cell slammed down.

The guards left, their footsteps disappearing along the corridor. There was a long, long silence and then a tiny, clicking, metallic noise: it was the sound of a key turning in a lock.

# TWENTY-ONE

'Well, here we all are,' exclaimed Ella, a minute or two later, after she had opened every door. 'It wasn't too difficult, stealing the key without being seen by a single one of the guards.'

Fidge and everyone else except the King had gathered in the centre of the circular room, and were standing in an awkward cluster next to the drinking fountain.

'Does this thing even work?' asked Graham, peering at it. He pressed a lever on the side, but no water came out of the spout. 'Pointless object,' he said.

'So, what next?' asked Ella. 'Now that I've managed to get us all out of the cells? Without being caught.'

'It wasn't just you,' said Graham. 'You couldn't have done it if the rest of us hadn't distracted the guards.'

'It was a team effort,' said Dr Carrot, firmly. 'Fine work from everybody.'

'I suppose what we do next is go upstairs and try and sneak out of the castle,' said Fidge, realizing, as she spoke, that too much time had been spent discussing how to get the key, and not enough in planning what to do afterwards. 'Perhaps there won't be too many guards around at night,' she added, hopefully.

The Pink raised a hand.

'Let me be first to climb the stair
I'll see how many guards are there.'

'OK,' said Fidge. 'That's very brave of you.'

'Us Pinks face danger with a shrug
If someone first gives us a hug.'

It smiled and held out its arms invitingly, and Fidge was just about to take a very reluctant step forward when someone tapped her on the shoulder. She turned to see the king.

'I can't remember,' he said, yawning, 'if I mentioned
About the secret tunnel? Denshened.'

'No,' said Fidge, stepping back sharply from the Pink Wimbley. 'You didn't.'

'Oh sorry, yes, I meant to say.
I'll open it, without delay.
It comes out just above the moat.'

There was a pause, while he took off his crown.

'Oh giddle gaddle goddle goat,' he added, casually, turning the crown upside down and placing it in the drinking fountain.

Each of the five points fitted into a slot in the bottom of the basin. There was a click, and a portion of wall swung open, revealing the mouth of an unlit tunnel.

In the moment of stunned silence that followed, they all heard the sound of someone coming down the stairs to the dungeons.

'Quick,' hissed Fidge, 'let's go. Can you close it afterwards?' she asked the king. 'Unless you've changed your mind, and you want to come?'

He shook his head, and she followed the others into blackness.

The secret door slammed shut behind them.

The tunnel sloped downwards, with occasional unexpected steps, so that the sound of cautious progress was punctuated with thuds and cries of pain as one or other of them tripped over.

'It seems to be widening,' called Dr Carrot from the front. 'I suggest that we whisper from now on. If we're near the exit then there may be g—'

There was a sudden crash.

'Ow,' said Dr Carrot. 'I appear to have rolled into a door.'

'There's no handle!' It was Graham, panic in his voice. 'We're trapped.'

Fidge fumbled her way past the others to the front of the line, and ran her hands across the wooden slab.

'Maybe it opens outwards,' she said. 'Let's all give it a shove at the same time.'

'Us Greys can't shove or push or strain
Our strongest muscle is our brain.'

'Everyone except the Grey,' said Fidge, putting her shoulder to the door. 'On the count of three. *One*—'

'I'm getting a panic attack, I'll have to sit down,' said Graham.
'*Two*—'

'I'm afraid, darling, that I'm not really able to push since I injured my back on the circus skills course.'

'*Three!!!*'

Fidge, aided by the Pink and Dr Carrot, gave a great heave and the entire door shifted, teetered for a second or two and then fell over with an enormous CRASH, revealing a darkened hillside.

'Hinges must have rusted,' said Fidge. 'I hope no one heard that.'

Mild grass-scented air spilled into the tunnel, and Graham stumbled out, breathing deeply.

'The moat's just down here,' he said.

The moon was half-hidden behind a cloud, but the water glinted faintly, like crumpled foil. The prisoners groped their way to the bank, and Fidge crouched down and dipped a hand in the water.

'Really cold,' she said. 'I wonder how deep it is.'

'Can't we use the drawbridge?' asked Graham.

'It was crawling with guards. Hang on, there's a branch on the ground here.' Fidge lowered it into the moat, and then kept lowering it until her whole arm was immersed, but still she couldn't touch the bottom. 'Who can swim?' she asked, looking round. 'Besides me, I mean.'

No one put their hand up.

Fidge looked back at the moat. Even in the dim light, she could see a row of trees on the far side, their branches moving gently – it wouldn't be much of a swim, no further than a length at her local pool.

'There's a saying: "He travels fastest who travels alone",' said Dr Carrot, quietly. 'It would be quite understandable if you decided to escape by yourself. No one would blame you.'

'I would,' said Graham, instantly. 'It's your fault I'm here in the first place so you're duty-bound to help me.'

'Darling,' said Ella, 'you must make your own decision,

but if you choose to go, then I and the Pink *demand* a group hug first.'

Graham snorted. 'You'll be lucky. Fidge never hugs anyone.'

Fidge threw him a stony glance and then stood, hesitating. The Grey cleared its throat.

'You've realized,' it said, 'that without a boat
We really cannot cross this moat.'

'Yes,' said Graham. 'Duh.'

'But I've been thinking, as Greys do,
And I have an idea for you.
A quick solution for our plight
So we can all escape this night.'

'Great,' said Fidge. 'What is it?'

'While others run around, Greys *think*
And forge solutions, link by link.
So answers gradually evolve
That "would", if used, our problem solve.'

'This is exactly what it was doing in the Punishments Room,' said Graham. 'Just going on and on and on and never getting to the point. Just *tell us.*'

'*Please,*' added Dr Carrot, reprovingly.

The Grey spoke again, slightly huffily this time.

'I rather hoped you'd understood
The door you broke is made of—'

'Wood!' shouted Fidge and Graham simultaneously, and just as they shouted, the moon shifted from behind a cloud and flooded the landscape with silver light. They could see the moat, curling round the base of the hillside like a broad ribbon, they could see the drawbridge, just a few hundred metres away, and the castle, looming above them, every detail sharp. They could also see a large number of guards, standing on the battlements. And the guards were staring in their direction, and shouting and pointing.

'Look at us!' said Fidge, in horror. 'We're all lit up!'

'How fabulously dramatic – it's the glitter!' said Ella, who looked as if she was draped in fairy lights.

And now they could all hear the rumble of the castle gate beginning to open.

'Come on!' shouted Fidge, running towards the fallen door. They slid and dragged it down towards the moat, and it slithered into the water and bobbed to the surface. They scrambled on, Ella at one end, everybody else at the other.

'And now paddle with your hands,' ordered Fidge. '*Paddle!*'

They could see the Blue guards hurrying down the slope towards them.

'I can't swim,' said Graham, sounding half-crazed with

nerves. 'The water's freezing, there's no life jacket, there's no armbands, there's no life guard, it's dark, I don't even have a coat, this craft is dangerously overloaded—'

'And yet, here you are, paddling with vigour,' said Dr Carrot, who was lying on her back in the middle of the door. 'I, for one, think that you've made tremendous progress.'

Guards were pouring out of the castle and the front-runners had nearly reached the moat, but the door and its sparkling passengers were now mid-stream. The Blues halted momentarily, and then turned and began running towards the drawbridge.

Fidge glanced at the woods on the far bank. The treetops were thrashing in the wind, casting odd shadows across the water.

'Not much further,' she said. 'Ella, can you reach out with your trunk, and try and pull us in to land?'

'Of course, darling. I was just thinking how lucky we are with the weather. A balmy night and not a breath of wind.'

'But—' Fidge, frowning, looked up at the trees again – the waving branches, the odd shadows. The very odd shadows.

'Nearly there,' said Ella, reaching out to grab a small sapling, and then losing her balance as it ripped straight out of the ground. She fell backwards, landing on Dr Carrot and knocking everyone else except Graham, into the black waters of the moat.

# TWENTY-TWO

Fidge surfaced and trod water, gasping at the cold. Just beside her, the Grey floated on its back, looking irritated but calm.

'The Pink Wimbley sank like a stone,' shouted Graham. 'Right beside you, somewhere.'

Fidge took a deep breath and dived, thrashing her hands around in the inky water, touching and then grasping a rubbery hand. 'Got it!' she gasped, surfacing, dragging the Pink with her. She could hear, from not too far away, the snapping of undergrowth and the bark of orders. 'The Blues have crossed the drawbridge,' she said, breathlessly, as she struggled to haul the Pink onto the bank. 'I don't think we're going to make it.'

And then, from a branch directly above her, a voice spoke. Unbelievably loudly.

'Now listen, chaps, I'll count to ten
And that will be the signal when
We launch our secret Green attack
To try and get our country back.'

'Oh *no*,' said Graham, helping Dr Carrot off the door and onto the mossy bank. 'It's the Greens again.'

Fidge was staring upwards; the trees were full of leaping Wimblies, and as the first Blues came into sight, sprinting through the ferny undergrowth, a cluster of Greens, all with the letter 'A' chalked on their backs, abseiled to the ground and struck Kung-fu-style poses. The voice spoke again.

'Now while Team "A" defends this zone
Team "B" can strike out on its own
And with stealth, secrecy and skill
Can cross the bridge and climb the hill.'

'Oh, *genius*,' said Graham, sarcastically, as the sprinting Blues instantly turned round and headed back towards the bridge.

'But this is our chance!' hissed Fidge. 'Let's get away!'

'We'll have to hurry,' said Dr Carrot, trundling through the bracken. 'I don't think it will be long before the Blue guards win this particular battle.'

'But what marvellous voice control those Greens have,' said Ella. 'Such projection! I rather suspect they're *professionally* trained.'

They emerged from the shelter of the wood and saw ahead of them a hay meadow, striped with shadow.

'Where are we going?' asked Graham, stopping dead. 'I'm not just wandering aimlessly, waiting to get caught again – where's the safest place to go?'

The Grey raised a hand.

'For those of us who think, not do
The answer's obvious and true.
There's just one place the Blues abhor;
They never venture past the door.
They'd much prefer to waste their days
On sports and games. Unlike us Greys.'

It paused.

'Just say it,' said Graham, through gritted teeth. 'Just say the answer quickly. *Say* it.'

'Or what about *miming* it?' suggested Ella.

Slightly frostily, the Grey took an imaginary book from a shelf and started reading.

'The library!' shouted Graham.

It nodded, grudgingly.

Fidge glanced over her shoulder; she could still hear the grunts and thuds of distant fighting. The thought of hiding away and wasting yet more time was more than she could stand; didn't the others realize that the situation was *urgent*? Didn't they understand that Minnie was waiting?

'OK, let's split up,' she said. 'You all go to the library, and start working on what the rest of that prophecy means, and I'll try and find Minnie's mobile phone. I think I might have seen it already – when I was standing on top of that column in the town square, I remember noticing some bright pink lights flashing, just like the ones on the phone. They looked miles away, though – near a sort of giant wheel.'

'That's Wimbley Fair,' said the Pink, 'I know the way
And since you saved my life today
*Please* let me stay and be your guide
And face all dangers by your side.'

The Pink looked at Fidge beseechingly, eyes wide, mouth stretched in an uncertain smile.

'OK,' said Fidge, surprised at how pleased she felt at the prospect of company. 'Thanks very much. No time for hugs,' she added, quickly, as the Pink lunged forward. 'We ought to get as far as we can under cover of darkness.'

The six of them set off across the moonlit meadow, following a path that took them across one stile and then another, past hedgerows starred with pale flowers, and alongside a stream that twisted briskly between steep banks. And then, at the corner of a maize field, the path split into two.

'The parting of the ways,' said Ella. 'Best of luck, darlings. Remember to breathe from the abdomen and always trust your innermost feelings.'

'Don't do anything rash,' added Dr Carrot. 'Take time to think before you act, and if in doubt, the best course is always to be polite.'

The Grey started to say something, paused, glanced at Ella and then gave a double thumbs-up.

'Bye,' said Graham. 'Hope you have wapid success in your search. And when I say wapid, I mean weally, weally, wapid.'

Fidge's mouth fell open – was Graham (spoiled, humour-less, selfish, terrified, arrogant Graham) actually trying to make her smile? She was so stunned that she could only manage a small nod in reply, and then she turned to follow the path, and the Pink hurried to catch her up. There was silence for a while, apart from the soft pad of their footsteps, and then Fidge felt the Wimbley's hand steal into hers. And though it belonged to something that looked like a glossy dustbin, it felt warm and reassuring, almost as if her mum were walking alongside her. Or even her dad.

# TWENTY-THREE

Dawn was breaking as Fidge and the Pink neared the fairground. Fidge was so tired that she felt as if her legs belonged to someone else, but she halted beside a nearby stream and splashed her face and felt instantly more awake. Up ahead, she could see the big wheel silhouetted against a dappled sky; next to it towered the opening span of a rollercoaster, the row of little cars sitting motionless at the top.

'I love rollercoasters,' said Fidge.

'It runs from here right back to town,' said the Pink.
'For most of it, you're upside down.'

'That's my favourite sort,' said Fidge. The entrance to the fairground lay just ahead, and three Orange Wimblies were already queueing outside the ticket office, despite the fact that it was hung with a banner which read:

### CLOSED UNTIL FURTHER NOTICE

Next to the office was a wooden turnstile. The Oranges watched, round-eyed, as Fidge and the Pink clambered over it, and then, with much giggling, they hurried across and followed the pair into the fairground.

The place was deserted, the carousel horses unridden, the dodgems unoccupied, the hook-a-ducks bobbing, unhooked, around their little river. The only noise was the creak of the big wheel gondalas as they swung in the breeze.

'We're looking for a mobile phone,' said Fidge, for the benefit of the Oranges, who were hanging around, staring at her and nudging each other. 'It's pink, covered with fake diamonds and it has a flashing lights display – and since I could see it from miles away, it's probably pretty big.' She was looking around as she spoke, glancing from the ghost train to the hall of mirrors, to the waltzer, but nothing caught her eye. 'It might be easier to spot it from above,' she said, glancing up at the big wheel. 'Maybe we can get that working, if the mechanism's not too complicated . . .'

The operator's booth was directly beneath the wheel; it contained a table, a chair, and a large, red ON/OFF switch.

'I'll manage that,' said the Pink, cheerfully. 'Just clamber in
And hold on tight – then I'll begin.
Unless you're gripped by fear or doubt
And first need hugs to sort that out?'

It looked at her hopefully.

'Afterwards,' said Fidge, swinging herself into the lowest
of the gondolas. It was quite large – easily big enough for two
Wimblies – and as she sat down, she saw one of the Oranges
ambling across, clearly keen on joining her.

'Quick,' she shouted to the Pink. 'Turn it on.'

There was a click, and a loud hum, and then the wheel
began, slowly, to turn. The Orange watched, crestfallen, as
Fidge rose out of reach; from her seat, she saw the Wimblies
shrinking to tiny dots, and the landscape opening up like the
page of a vast book. But a book would have straight edges,
and Wimbley Land was very clearly circular: the castle on
its hill right at the centre, the train track wiggling round it
and the surrounding fields a vivid green, fading abruptly to a
much paler colour at the horizon.

A much, *much* paler colour. Whitish, in fact.

*Odd*, thought Fidge.

She remembered suddenly what she was supposed to be
looking for, and dragged her attention back to the fairground,
her gaze darting over the patchwork of rides and attractions.
*Where on earth was Minnie's phone?* The wheel reached its
highest point, Fidge glanced up, momentarily, and there it

was! Exactly on her level: a mobile phone the size of a petrol pump, encrusted with plastic diamonds, twinkling with pink lights and lying back, like a lazy passenger, in the very first car of the rollercoaster.

'I can see it,' she shouted down to the Pink. 'It's on the . . .' Her voice died away. Not far behind the Pink Wimbley was the hall of mirrors, and behind *that* was a row of candy-floss and hamburger stalls and behind *those* was an open field – but instead of being green, the field and everything beyond it was the same weird, bleached-out shade that she'd just seen in the far, far distance, right on the other side of Wimbley Land. She stared, puzzled, but she was losing height now, and the view was disappearing. 'I'm going to go round again,' she shouted to the Pink. 'There's something really strange over there, behind the hall of mirrors. I want to have another look.'

She saw the Pink crane round curiously at where she was pointing, and then, as the wheel turned and began to rise again it called up to her.

'I'm going to see if something's wrong –
I'll hurry back and won't be long.'

It scampered off and Fidge turned again to the wider view. And this time, as she rose above the countryside, the oddness of it leaped out at her. It was as if Wimbley Land was a circular puddle of colour on a white floor. The fairground was situated just inside the puddle, and immediately beyond it, the world was milky-pale.

A line of verse slid into her head, a line that had been spoken by one of the Purples: *'When rage soaks up the joy and fun and colour out of everyone'.*

'Soaks up,' she repeated, out loud. Why did that image seem so familiar to her? Why did it seem so significant?

She jerked her attention back to the view; below her, the Pink was making its way past the hall of mirrors and towards the bleached field.

'Hang on,' she shouted. 'Let's go and look at it together.' But she was too far away to be heard. Her gondola reached the top of the big wheel and began to descend; she lost sight of the Pink behind the fairground rides.

'Hey!' she shouted at the Oranges standing below. 'Can you press the OFF switch? The red OFF switch?'

They gaped up at her, and then one of them started waving, happily.

'The OFF switch!' She shouted again, as the wheel returned her to ground level. The other two Oranges joined in the waving. For a third time, Fidge began to ascend above the fairground. Minnie's mobile phone swung into view again, and the row of snack stalls – and the Pink, who was standing with its back to her, staring out at the pale field.

She shouted until her voice was ragged, but the Pink didn't answer, or move, and then Fidge was heading back down again, and she knew that there was only one sure way of getting off the wheel. She stood up, and slung a leg over the side of the gondola, so that she was riding it like a horse. It swayed beneath her and she hung on, heart jumping. The ground grew nearer, and nearer. She waited until the last possible second and then swung the other leg over and dropped. She hit the ground hard, and rolled, and lay for a few moments, both ankles and one elbow throbbing, before slowly sitting up. Directly in front of her stood the three Oranges. They started clapping.

'Well thanks for your help,' said Fidge, sarcastically, rubbing her arm. She began to roll up her sleeve, and the clapping faltered to a stop. One of the Oranges took a shuddering gasp.

'What's the matter?' asked Fidge, examining the small graze on her elbow. It was bleeding slightly. She looked up.

The Wimblies were staring fixedly at the wound, their jaws sagging with horror.

'It's only a scrape,' said Fidge, slightly surprised. 'Look,' she added, sticking the elbow out towards them.

They reared backwards as if she'd lunged at them with a snake, and then bolted away across the fairground, screaming as they ran.

Fidge watched them disappear into the distance and then hauled herself to her feet and started walking, rather painfully, in search of the Pink.

# TWENTY-FOUR

Graham, Ella, Dr Carrot and the Oldest and Wisest of the Greys had reached the Wimbley Woo Library in the early hours of the morning, and Graham had fallen asleep, minutes later, on a large beanbag that he'd found in a comfortable reading area. He awoke to full daylight, the sound of his own stomach rumbling and the smell of toast.

The last time he'd eaten a piece of toast, he'd choked on a scratchy crumb and had been driven to casualty by his mother to have his throat checked; that had been a year and a half ago and since then, even the smell of it had been enough to make him cough.

Now, however, he was starving, and he followed his

nose to a small staffroom where Ella was eating a slice spread with butter.

'Good sleep?' she asked. 'Hungry?'

He nodded to both, and ate his way through four pieces of toast without so much as a single cough. Through the staffroom door he could see Dr Carrot and the Oldest and Wisest of the Greys standing together in a corner, apparently deep in conversation.

'I have to say that although I don't altogether share Dr Carrot's rather *rigid* stance on manners, I very much admire her listening skills,' said Ella. She picked up a marker pen with her trunk and turned to a large whiteboard. 'I've been working on the prophecy and I'd be very keen to hear the views of an intelligent and sensitive young man such as yourself.'

Graham nodded. He'd been missing the amount of praise that he normally got, and it was good to hear that he was properly appreciated. He stood in front of the board and read out loud.

> 'First seek the lost device and ring
> The listener who knows everything
> Then cast aside the words you use
> For summing up the Wimbley Woos
> And look again at every hue –
> A different word for each is true.
> Then team new weaknesses and skills
> To win the way to cure all ills.'

Underneath the poem, Ella had written:

| COLOUR | WORDS WE USE | DIFFERENT WORD |
|--------|--------------|----------------|
| BLUE | STRONG | |
| YELLOW | TIMID | |
| PURPLE | UNDERSTAND THE PAST/ FUTURE OF LAND | |
| PINK | GIVE CUDDLES | |
| ORANGE | SILLY/GET IN MUDDLES | |
| GREEN | DARING | |
| GREY | WISE AND RARELY WRONG | |

'I presume,' she said, twirling the pen, 'that when it says "*a different word for each is true*", it's saying that we have to look at the *whole* of each type of Wimbley, and appreciate its *range* of skills, rather than focus on the most obvious. I think that's rather a lovely message, don't you?'

'Mmm,' said Graham. 'Except that it says "weaknesses" as well as "skills", so the different word doesn't necessarily have to be something impressive or clever. For instance, I'd say that the most accurate "different" word for Blues is "greedy". They'll do anything for sweets. On the other hand, Yellows cycle everywhere, and they push Wed Wabbit round in that stupid buggy, so I'd say that the word for them is "fit". I haven't met any Purples yet.'

'Oh, they're marvellous,' said Ella. 'Very deep and mystical and tremendously . . .'

She paused and then wrote **THEATRICAL!** next to **PURPLE** on the chart. 'And of course,' she continued, 'we've discovered that Pinks are terribly "brave".' She wrote that too. 'I don't have any personal experience of Oranges,' she added.

'Me neither,' said Graham. 'Though they sound incredibly annoying.'

'What about Greens?'

'Loud,' said Graham, emphatically.

Ella nodded agreement before writing it down.

'And Greys?' she asked, eyeing the last colour on the list.

'I can actually think of two different words for Greys,' said Graham. 'They both begin with "B". The first one's "boring" and the second one's "buoyant".'

'Buoyant?'

'Yes, don't you remember – the Grey floated when it fell in the moat? The Pink sank and the Grey floated.'

'Let's put "buoyant" then, shall we?' said Ella. 'If one has a choice then it's always best to take the *positive* option.'

She had just finished writing, when Graham heard the squeak of wheels. Dr Carrot was approaching across the library, the Grey beside her.

'We've been having a very interesting discussion,' she said.

'*Really?*' asked Graham incredulously.

Dr Carrot gave him a hard look.

'Really?' he asked again, less sarcastically this time.

'I enquired how the current political situation arose,' she continued. 'And I now have the facts at my disposal, which I think it would be useful to share. Apparently it all began on the king's birthday, when he traditionally has a picnic.'

The Grey raised its hand.

'Except, of course, as I explained,
Three years ago, because it rained.'

'Thank you,' said Dr Carrot. 'Anyway, this year, the Wimblies decided to amuse the monarch with a giant game of Hide and Seek.'

The Grey raised a hand again.

'To get the facts all straight and true
Is something Greys prefer to do.
So I should like to make it clear
That Hide and Seek was my idea.'

'Thank you,' said Dr Carrot again, slightly less gratefully this time.

'This is going to take *for ever*,' muttered Graham.

'I have a wonderful idea,' announced Ella. She drew a line across the bottom of the whiteboard and handed the marker pen to the Grey. 'It would be so much more helpful if you could write your notes down as you go along, and then give them all to us at the end, so we can really *absorb* them.'

'Excellent thought,' said Dr Carrot.

Ella smiled modestly.

'Right,' continued the carrot. 'So a huge picnic rug was laid out just in front of the castle and covered in cakes and sweets and sandwiches, and on it was a note to tell the King that all the Wimbley Woos were hiding, and the picnic would begin when he'd found them. Unfortunately, when the King read that, he decided he wanted to have a little rest first, so he lay down and went to sleep.'

'Typical,' said Graham.

'All the Wimblies waited in their hiding places – the Yellows were in a large cornfield, the Greens were up trees and the Greys had gone for quite a clever idea—'

The Grey raised a hand.

'Notes at the end,' said Ella, brightly. 'Write it down.'

'—which was to hide on board the train. The Blues, meanwhile, had decided to hide very close to the picnic, so that the king would find them first, and then they'd be able to—'

'Eat all the sweets!' interrupted Graham.

'Correct. But' – Dr Carrot looked at them gravely – 'while the king was asleep, Wed Wabbit suddenly arrived at the castle.'

'Just the way that I suddenly arrived on a hillside, and Fidge suddenly arrived in a tunnel,' said Graham.

'And Wed Wabbit suggested to the Blues that they take all the sweets back to the castle to stop the other Wimblies from getting them. Since then, he's been using the Blues' greed to control the country.'

'But why?' asked Graham. 'What does he get out of it? OK, so he's the boss and the whole country's terrified of him and everyone rushes about obeying his orders, but he's stuck in the castle, he never gets out, he never *does* anything, or talks to anyone or has any fun or . . .' He suddenly became aware that Dr Carrot was looking at him in a significant way. '*What?*' he asked, defensively. 'You're not trying to say that's like me, are you?'

Dr Carrot remained silent, but Graham found himself blushing uncomfortably and he turned away from her gaze. 'Wonder where Fidge is,' he muttered. 'I might go and look out of the window, see if she's anywhere near.'

'I rather think there's something we need to do first,' said Ella, flicking a glance towards the Grey. It was standing, pointing at the whiteboard, which was completely covered in tiny, densely written notes.

With a groan, Graham began to listen.

# TWENTY-FIVE

Fidge limped through the fairground towards where she'd last seen the Pink.

She rounded the corner of the hall of mirrors, and though she'd been half-expecting it, the view was still startling.

Ahead of her, across a stretch of grass, and just beyond the row of food stalls, all colour stopped. It was as if the paint had suddenly run out: pallid trees, an ashen hedge, a meadow the colour of an overwashed white sheet. And standing with its back to Fidge, right on the line between blank and colour, was the Pink Wimbley – except that now it was pink-*tinged* rather than pink – the colour of a plastic toy that's been left in the sun for too long.

'Hey,' called Fidge, hobbling towards it. 'Are you OK?'

It turned slowly.

'Oh hi,' it said, tonelessly.

She waited for the rest of the rhyme, and when it didn't come, her heart gave a lurch. 'What's the matter?' she asked.

'Oh nothing. I was just thinking about whether it's time to read my gas meter.'

'*What?*'

'And my hedge needs trimming.'

'But we're on a quest to free Wimbley Land from the rule of Wed Wabbit! You went to prison because of it!'

'I ought to get home and boil-wash some tea towels first.' The round eyes were half closed with apparent boredom.

'But . . .' Fidge cast desperately around for something that might restore the Pink to its usual self. 'But when we free Wimbley Land, everyone will want to hug you. You'll get loads and loads of hugs. Won't that be great?'

'No,' said the Pink, listlessly. 'I don't really like hugs.'

Fidge stared at it, shocked. She tried to work out what was going on, but her brain was feeling oddly sluggish. In fact her whole body felt weighty and peculiar, as if she was growing roots, and her thoughts seemed to be stuck in the same, dull place.

*I ought to get away from here,* she thought, staring at the monochrome landscape, *but I don't know whether I can be bothered. Maybe I'll just stand and think about whether I ought to open a high-interest savings account or not. Maybe I should read a leaflet on the financial services available in this branch.*

And then, distantly, she heard a noise: a tinny, electronic, irritating, utterly familiar noise.

NING **NANG** NINGETY **NANG** NINGETY NINGETY **NANG**

It was the unmistakable ring tone of Minnie's toy mobile, and it seemed to jerk Fidge back to herself again.

NING **NANG** NINGETY **NANG** NINGETY NINGETY **NANG**

She took a step backwards, and it was like ungluing herself from waist-deep mud. 'Come on, we need to get away,' she said, urgently, grabbing the Pink's hand and half-dragging it across the grass and past the hall of mirrors.

'Can I go home and descale the kettle?' asked the Pink.

'No time,' said Fidge. She hauled the Wimbley as far as the entrance to the rollercoaster, and then let go of its hand. 'Wait for me, OK?'

She looked up, craning her head back; the six linked cars of the rollercoaster were parked near the top of the first long slope, the front car just inches from a near-vertical downward swoop. 'Hope the brake's on,' she muttered, and then stepped over the barrier labelled DANGER, DO NOT STEP OVER THIS BARRIER and began to walk up the track.

Her feet thudded solidly on the wooden struts. It was

an easy, gradual climb, not frightening as long as she avoided looking down at the growing drop. The phone stopped ringing just as she'd reached the last of the six cars, and she steadied herself and turned round to look at the view. What she saw made her turn cold: Wimbley Land was shrinking. In the few minutes since she'd last seen it, the Whiteness had crept onward, swallowing up the candyfloss stalls and advancing as far as the hall of mirrors. And as she stared, she realized that she could actually *see* the colour disappearing, inch by steady inch. It reminded her of something – something she'd seen, not long ago, in another world. *It reminded her of the pool of spilled orange juice being soaked up by Wed Wabbit in Minnie's bedroom.*

'It's him,' she said, with absolute certainty. 'He's doing it.'

The phone started to ring again, and she began to scramble from one car to the next, popcorn and scattered crisps crunching under her feet. By the time she reached the front one, the noise was almost deafening, and she crammed herself into the seat beside the vast mobile and thumped the sparkling purple button marked ANSWER.

The ringing stopped abruptly.

'Hello? Is anyone there?' she asked, into the silence.

'It's me,' replied a little voice, and Fidge felt as if someone had reached into her chest and punched her heart. For a long moment she couldn't manage to say anything at all and when she at last spoke, her throat was so tight that her voice was a husky mutter.

'Oh, Minnie.'

'You're all cwackly.'

'Yes, I'm . . . it's a bad line,' said Fidge. She took a deep breath; her whole body was trembling. 'Are you really all right?' She asked. All she could think of was the terrible smash and thud of the accident.

'I bwoke my leg and I banged my head.'

'It was my fault,' said Fidge.

'It wasn't. I didn't look wight and then I didn't look left.'

'But . . .'

'I had some medicine to stop it hurting, but I need Wed Wabbit to make me all better. When are you bwinging him?'

Fidge struggled to find an answer. 'Soon. As soon as I possibly can. Listen, Minnie, I have to ask you something. How do I get—'

'But I'm talking to *Fidge*,' said Minnie, interrupting, her voice a little distant, as if she'd just turned her head. 'I'm pwetending the wemote contwol's a phone. Do you want to talk to her?'

There was a pause, and then someone else said, 'Hello Fidge.'

It was her mum. And to hear that ordinary, lovely voice in this strange and dangerous world was almost painful.

'Yes, she's longing to see you too,' continued Fidge's mum, who was well-practised at having imaginary phone conversations, 'and of course she's desperate to get Wed Wabbit back as well, so tell Auntie Ruth to get here as soon as she can. Have you had your lunch?'

I can't answer, thought Fidge. I can't talk at all, because if my mum hears my voice coming out of a television remote control, she'll think she's gone mad.

'Ooh that sounds nice,' said her mum, as if listening to Fidge chattering away. 'With custard? Lovely. Well, I'll hand you back to Minnie now. Bye lovely girl, see you very, very soon.'

And Fidge mouthed the word 'bye' and gave her eyes a swipe because her vision was suddenly rather blurry.

'Hello,' said her little sister again. 'There's a telly on a bendy arm just by my bed.'

'Listen, Minnie,' said Fidge, urgently, before Minnie could go off on another topic, 'you've got to talk to me about Wed Wabbit. Tell me everything you know about him.'

'About Wed Wabbit?'

'Yes.'

'Well . . . He's a wabbit.'

'Yes.'

'And he's wed.'

'Yes. And . . . ?'

'I might watch a DVD now. They've got *Fwozen*.'

'Hang on. Hang on just a few seconds.' Fidge rubbed her forehead, and tried to think quickly. 'OK. What if – just imagine this, Minnie, pretend it's a proper story, like in a book we're reading – what if Wed Wabbit went to Wimbley Land? What if he made himself king and bossed everybody around and formed the Blues into his army and soaked up all the colours? What would you do?'

'I'd have a little word with him.'

'But what if he was as big as a house?'

'I'd have a BIG word with him.'

'But how would you fight the Blues?'

'I wouldn't fight them. I don't like fighting, I like playing games.'

Fidge nearly groaned; this was absolutely hopeless. She realized that she'd been relying on Minnie to instantly solve everything, somehow forgetting that her sister was a) recovering from a serious road accident and b) four years old. She had to approach the whole thing differently.

'OK, just imagine that *I* was in Wimbley Land as well. Imagine I was stuck there with Wed Wabbit. How would we both get home to you and Mum again?'

There was a pause.

'By bus,' said Minnie, decisively. 'A big silver bus with pink wheels like the one I've got at home. But you're not stuck, are you?'

'No,' lied Fidge.

'And Wed Wabbit's not stuck either, is he?' Minnie's voice began to tremble.

'No,' lied Fidge again.

'I don't want him to be stuck, I want him back.' Her sister started crying. 'I want Wed Wabbit, he'll be all sad and lonely without me.'

'I'll get him,' said Fidge, 'I promise.'

'But I want him back. I want my Wed Wabbit, *I want my Wed—*'

And there was a click and the line went dead.

Fidge groaned with frustration and punched the purple glittery button again, but nothing came from the phone but a faint hiss. Panic was beginning to ripple through her. The conversation with Minnie hadn't yielded a single useful answer, and without answers, how could she get back home again? And then, through the panic, a single, chilling thought emerged: she'd been in Wimbley Land for two whole days, but back in the real world, no time had passed at all. Her mum hadn't been anxiously wondering where she was because her mum hadn't even noticed that she'd gone.

*Which means*, thought Fidge, *that I could be trapped in Wimbley Land for twenty years, or a hundred years, or for all eternity and no one, no one, would ever miss me.*

She had never felt so terrified, or so alone, and she was struck by a sudden, desperate wish to see the others again – Ella, Dr Carrot, even *Graham* . . .

From far below, she heard voices, and she peered over the side of the car and then immediately ducked down again. A Blue patrol was marching through the fairground; if they saw her, she'd be arrested and dragged off to jail again. She crouched, silent, hardly daring to breathe.

And then the phone rang.

## NING **NANG** NINGETY **NANG** NINGETY NINGETY **NANG**

Even as Fidge thumped the button, she could see that the

Blues had stopped dead and were looking up at her.

Minnie's voice wailed out of the speaker. 'I want my Wed Wabbit, please, Fidge, bwing me Wed Wabbit!'

The Blues were already sprinting to the rollercoaster, and within seconds the two fastest had vaulted the barrier and started climbing up the track, blocking any chance of escape.

Minnie was really sobbing now, her voice weak and wild. Fidge could hear her mother anxiously calling for a nurse.

'I'll get him for you, Minnie, I promise,' said Fidge. 'I promise.' She peered over the side of the car and saw the Pink standing on the ground below. It was staring drearily into space, oblivious to all the noise.

'Turn it on!' She shouted. 'Turn on the rollercoaster! Didn't you say it goes right back to town?'

The Pink gaped up at her.

'I ought to go and tidy my shed,' it said.

'Please,' shouted Fidge, with desperation.

The Blues were halfway up the track and she could hear their angry shouts.

'Oh *please*. This is so tiny compared to all the huge, brave things you've done already. Just go and press the ON button. And *then* you can tidy your shed!'

Slowly, the Pink nodded. Slowly, it turned and disappeared into the operating booth of the rollercoaster.

The Blues were nearly at the last car now.

'Fidge!' Called Minnie. 'Fidge!!'

'What is it, Minnie?'

The car jerked forward with a ratcheting sound. There was a shout of frustration from the Blues.

'It's weally, weally, weally important. When you find Wed Wabbit, you've got to give him—'

The car gave a lurch and with a noise like a million marbles being tipped down a staircase, it roared down the slope.

'What?' shouted Fidge, clinging on with one hand, her other arm flung across the phone to act as a seatbelt. 'Give him *what?*'

But the drop was too steep. Minnie's mobile tipped forward over her arm, and fell through the air, its lights still twinkling. It turned an elegant somersault, hit the ground and smashed into a thousand pieces.

Fidge yelled – a yell of rage, of frustration, of misery – and she went on yelling, the fairground blurring beneath her. The car climbed and twisted and then dropped again, throwing her through one corkscrew turn after another, the sky and the ground changing places, her stomach dancing around somewhere near her neck. And then she was the right way up again, and the track had become a long, gently sloping descent that curved lazily around a sports field and an outdoor swimming pool, and juddered to a halt at the end of a street of striped and spotted houses on the outskirts of Wimbley Town.

Fidge climbed out on shaky legs. A curtain twitched in one of the houses and she glimpsed a Yellow Wimbley looking fearfully out at her. Two Oranges were sitting on a nearby garden wall, and as she wavered across to them, still dizzy after the journey, they nudged each other and dissolved into the usual giggles.

'Which way's the library?' she asked, too tired for politeness.

The giggles continued.

'If you don't tell me where it is,' said Fidge, wearily, 'then I'll just have to show you the graze on my elbow.' She began to roll up her sleeve. Instantly, both Oranges stopped laughing and pointed left.

'Thanks,' she said, and trudged off, yawning.

# TWENTY-SIX

Fidge woke, and for a moment – a wonderful moment – she thought she was in her own bed. And then came a squeak of wheels and she opened her eyes to see Dr Carrot rolling across Wimbley Library towards her, accompanied by Graham.

'You're right,' said Graham, glumly. 'There's a roof terrace upstairs and this morning, after you told us about all the colour disappearing, we went up and looked and we couldn't see anything, but we've just been up again and this time it's visible. A thick white line all along the horizon. So whatever it is, it's getting closer.'

Fidge sat up, blinking. 'How long have I been asleep then?' She asked.

'Hours and hours. It's nearly sunset.'

She rubbed her eyes and stretched. When she'd arrived at the library she'd been so tired that after a couple of sentences of explanation she'd noticed a pile of beanbags in the corner and had found herself going over there just to have a little sit down. The next second, she'd been fast asleep, and now another whole day had disappeared.

'Tea?' asked Ella, noticing that she was awake. 'Toast?'

'Yes please.'

'Come and have a look at what we've been doing,' said Graham, pointing to the whiteboard. 'There's just one word missing.'

| COLOUR | WORDS WE USE | DIFFERENT WORD |
|--------|-------------|----------------|
| BLUE | STRONG | GREEDY |
| YELLOW | TIMID | FIT |
| PURPLE | UNDERSTAND THE PAST/ FUTURE OF LAND | THEATRICAL! |
| PINK | GIVE CUDDLES | BRAVE |
| ORANGE | SILLY/GET IN MUDDLES | |

| GREEN | DARING | LOUD |
|-------|--------|------|
| GREY | WISE AND RARELY WRONG | BUOYANT |

Fidge picked up the pen and wrote Squeamish in the blank space beside ORANGE.

The others looked at her, puzzled.

'Honestly,' she said, 'they're terrified by the sight of blood.' She looked again at the prophecy written at the top of the board. 'Isn't there a bit missing from the end of that? Wasn't there a line about doing something difficult?'

Ella nodded, and took the scroll from her skirt pocket. 'It says:

And finally, just one of you
Must find the hardest thing to do
And when it's done – and only then –
You'll find your way back home again.'

'The hardest thing?' repeated Graham. 'Well, what's that? Climbing Everest? Working out the diameter of the sun?'

'I suppose it depends on the person,' said Fidge. 'What's hard for one person might be easy for another.'

'A good observation,' commented Dr Carrot.

'Well, let's not bother with that until we've worked out

everything else,' said Graham. He looked at Fidge. 'You did manage to find the phone, didn't you?'

She nodded.

'And did you speak to dear Minnie?' asked Ella.

Fidge nodded again, more reluctantly this time.

'How is she?'

'Well, she's quite upset, she wants Wed Wabbit back. She's missing him really badly.'

'But she gave you some answers, didn't she?' asked Graham.

Fidge hesitated as the memory of her useless conversation came sliding back, and when she spoke, it was in a mumble. 'I asked her what to do about Wed Wabbit.'

'And what did she say?'

'She said . . . she said we should have a little word with him.'

'*WHAT*?' shouted Graham.

'That's the phrase our mum always uses when she's going to tell someone off. And I asked how we could fight the Blues. And Minnie said that she didn't like fighting, she liked playing games. And then I asked her how we could get back home again. And she said . . .' Fidge swallowed. 'She said we should get the bus. And she told me that when we found Wed Wabbit, we had to give him something.'

'Give him what?' demanded Graham.

'I don't know. That's when the phone broke.'

There was a pause, and then Graham lay down full-length on the floor.

'Could I enquire what you are doing?' asked Dr Carrot.

'I'm going to lie here until either somebody rescues me or I *die*. Whichever comes first.'

'Minnie's only four,' said Fidge, defensively. 'And she's not well. She didn't really understand the situation.'

'Well maybe that's because you didn't explain it properly.'

'Yes I did! I suppose you think you could have done better, like you do about *everything*.'

'I can't help being intelligent. I'm not going to apologize for it.'

'What would you have asked Minnie, then?'

'I'd have asked her to suggest a strategy.'

'Have you ever *met* a four year old?'

'I imagine that they're not very different from you.'

'Says the person who's lying on the floor having a *tantrum*!'

A loud chinking sound cut through the shouting and Fidge turned to see Ella hitting a teacup with a spoon.

'Now, darlings, let's not argue,' she said. 'Especially when you're *both* right.'

'Huh?' Said Graham and Fidge, simultaneously.

'Graham's correct in that we need a strategy, but Fidge's wonderful questions have provided us with exactly that.'

Fidge and Graham exchanged a baffled glance.

'It's all in the interpretation,' said Dr Carrot. 'We are clearly required to have a serious discussion with Wed Wabbit, but if we go anywhere near him, we'll be arrested by his Guards. We can't fight the Blues – they're too strong and too numerous – so instead we need to use Minnie's suggestion to distract them from their job.'

'What, you mean we should play *games* with the Blues?' asked Fidge, uncertainly. 'What sort of games?'

'Team games,' suggested Ella. 'After all, the prophecy tells us to *"team new weaknesses and skills"*.'

'Team games with sweets as prizes,' added Graham. 'We know Blues are greedy. We could use that greediness to lure them away from the castle.'

'But we can't get any sweets,' said Fidge. 'They're all locked away in the Rewards Room.'

'True,' said Dr Carrot.

There was a long, long pause while they all thought about it. Ella flapped her ears, Graham looked at the floor, Fidge looked at the ceiling, Dr Carrot did some squeaky, on-the-spot manouevres. And then the Oldest and Wisest of the Greys cleared its throat.

'Since "thinking" is the thing Greys do,
My thoughts have raced ahead of you
And worked out that we can't begin
If we've no sweets for those who win.'

'Genius,' said Graham, sarcastically.

'Unless,' continued the Grey, ignoring him,

'we can detain the Blues

By making sure they always lose.'

'Genius!' said Graham, again, but this time his tone was quite different, and his expression – usually a cross between irritation and misery – was suddenly alight, as if there were fireworks going off behind his eyes. 'Don't you get it?' he asked the others, crossing rapidly over to the whiteboard. 'We've worked out all the different words for Wimblies so what we need now are team games that *make use* of those different words. So, for instance, Yellows are really fit, so if they competed against the Blues in a cycling race, then the Yellows would be certain to win.'

Fidge stared at him, open mouthed, hope stirring inside her.

'Oh, but that's marvellous!' exclaimed Ella. 'And the Purples are theatrical so they could challenge the Blues to charades!'

'And Pinks are brave,' said Fidge, 'so they'd be good at something like dares. And Greys float, so they could have a swimming contest. We'd have to get them off the train first, of course . . .'

'They're only stuck on it because none of them can operate the brake – not because it's jammed or anything, but because they can only "think" not "do",' said Graham. 'We were told all about it earlier. In incredible detail.' He flicked his eyes towards the Grey, and mouthed the words *two hour lecture* at Fidge.

'OK,' she said, 'well, maybe if we—'

'Blues!' called Dr Carrot, sharply. 'I can hear them talking.'

In the momentary hush, they could hear the harsh, deep gurgling tones of the guards coming from just outside.

'I thought they never went near the library,' whispered Fidge, and then she heard the outer door opening. There was no time to run, or hide. The five of them stood frozen as a troop of Blues marched in.

Except, they didn't march, they drifted, slowly and aimlessly.

And they weren't blue, they were only blue*ish*, the colour of an early morning sky. The only things that hadn't faded were their sashes which looked, if anything, a darker, nastier red than before.

One of the guards wandered up to Fidge. She took an instinctive step back.

'Do you have a book about different types of shoe polish?' It asked.

Fidge shook her head, her eyes sliding towards the other four guards. One of them had picked up a leaflet on careers in banking, while another was staring at the floor.

'That carpet needs a bit of a Hoover,' it said, dully.

'I think this must be the patrol I saw at the fairground,' muttered Fidge. 'The same thing's happened to them, as happened to the Pink.' And she wondered, with a tweak of sadness, whether her companion was still standing next to the big wheel, or whether it had found a shed to tidy.

'They've stopped rhyming,' said Graham.

'They've stopped *living*,' added Ella.

'It nearly happened to me too,' said Fidge. 'I felt as if I was stuck in concrete and all I could think about was boring things like bank accounts. If I'd stayed at the border any longer, I think I'd have ended up like *them*.'

'But that border's getting closer all the time!' said Graham. 'If it catches up with us we might as well be dead. And even if we manage to have a word with Wed Wabbit, how's that going to stop all the colour disappearing?'

'Because it's Wed Wabbit who's *making* the colours disappear,' said Fidge. 'He's like a giant sponge, soaking it all up – it's just like the Purple said.'

'*When rage soaks up the joy and fun and colour out of everyone,*' said Ella. 'Yes, Fidge is right. We have to talk to him and stop him.'

'Fast,' added Graham. 'Really, really fast.'

'Then we need to come up with a detailed plan,' said Dr Carrot. 'And we have to explain that plan to every non-Blue Wimbley in the country. We must have a public meeting.'

'But won't the Blues come and break it up?'

The Grey raised a hand.

'Please, darling,' said Ella, 'in the rather urgent circumstances, can you make an extra special effort to be brief?'

The Grey closed its eyes and appeared to think hard.

'There are no Blue patrols at night,' it said, with an effort. 'They're in the castle, locked up tight.'

'You see!' exclaimed Ella. 'That was terribly impressive and helpful. And where would you suggest we hold an extremely large after-dark meeting? In that fabulously short way you've just discovered.'

The Grey appeared to blush slightly.

'There's room for all
In our Town Hall.'

'Urk,' it added, as Ella enfolded it in a huge, congratulatory hug.

'We know what to do,' said Dr Carrot. 'Let's get on with it.'

# TWENTY-SEVEN

It was after midnight, and all over Wimbley Land, scurrying figures were whispering beneath hedgerows, cycling silently through the darkness, knocking softly on doors, and waiting for clouds to ease across the moon, before darting through the deep-shadowed lanes.

Apart from the Greens, who were bellowing to everyone within a half-mile radius about the exact time and location of the meeting, and the Oranges, who were running in circles, shrieking with excitement.

For more than an hour, a river of Wimblies poured into the town, along the narrow main street and up the steps of the Town Hall. Fidge, waiting at the side of the stage, saw the huge room gradually become a shifting sea of colour, the

175

Yellows clustering nervously around the exit doors, the Pinks with their arms around one another, the Oranges revolving slowly, fixed and idiotic grins on their faces, the Purples standing in a fog of incense, humming slightly, eyes half-closed, and the Greens practising free-climbing up the coat hooks at the back.

And when the street was at last empty and the hall full, Fidge bolted the outer doors against unwelcome visitors, and joined the others on the stage.

The Grey held up a hand for silence, and the restless murmur of the audience died to a rustle of whispers, followed by an ear-crushing shout from the coat hooks:

> 'We mustn't make our speakers wait,
> So quiet, all, and concentrate!'

'Thank you,' said Dr Carrot, wheeling forwards. 'What I am about to say is very serious, so I would be grateful for your full attention. Wimbley Land is under threat, not just from the dictatorship of Wed Wabbit' – there was a stir of panic from the Yellows – 'but also from something else, something new and urgent, as our colleague Fidge here will illustrate for you. *Try and keep it low-key,*' she added to Fidge, in a whisper. '*We need to inform, not scare.*'

Fidge walked nervously to the front, holding a corkboard onto which she'd pinned a map of Wimbley Land. Taking a marker pen, she drew a circle on it, with the castle at the centre. 'Inside this circle,' she said, 'Wimbley Land still looks quite normal. Outside it, though, all the colour's disappearing from the landscape, and what's slightly worrying is—'

An orange hand shot up at the back of the hall and waggled frantically.

'Yes?' asked Fidge.

'We're not too sure of what you mean,
Or where it is, or what you've seen
To help us try and understand
Please use a map of Wimbley Land.'

'But I *am* using a map,' said Fidge.

Behind her, Graham stood on a chair and peered out at the audience, before giving a grunt of frustration.

'The Oranges are all facing the back of the room,' he muttered. 'Just ignore them.'

'As I was saying,' said Fidge. 'What's worrying is—'

This time, the hand that shot up was pink.

'What is it?' asked Fidge, already guessing what was coming.

'As Orange heads are in a muddle
I think that what they need's a cuddle.'

'Can I finish this first?' said Fidge, but the Pinks were already making their way through the crowd towards the Oranges. The noise level rose.

'If you can just try and *listen*,' continued Fidge, 'the really worrying thing is—'

'What you are saying is unclear.
We're at the back. We cannot hear.'

'OK,' said Fidge, raising her voice to a near-shout of frustration. 'What's completely *terrifying* is that the normal bit of Wimbley Land is shrinking and anyone who goes near the edge gets all the colour and personality totally sucked out of them!!!'

There was a huge, collective gasp of horror. Fidge's gaze met a sea of boggling eyes.

'I didn't mean to scare you,' she said, uncertainly. 'But that's what's happening.'

There was instant chaos: screaming, hysterical laughter, shouts, wails and the thuds of fainting Yellows.

'Woe!' chanted the Purples, starting to dance in a circle, waving scarves.

'Woe! Woe to all in Wimbley Land.
As colours fade and life turns bland.
So surely this will be the doom
Of every Wimbley in this room.'

'But we've got a really good plan!' shouted Fidge. 'If you'd just listen . . .'

Three Oranges had got stuck in the exit door, and the Yellows were piling up behind them, and the Greens were bellowing for them to move, and panic seemed to have filled the hall like smoke.

Fidge turned, shamefaced, to her companions.

'Sorry,' she said. 'That went a bit wrong.'

It was Ella who stepped forward, arms outstretched, trunk raised, her voice mellow and rich and radiating authority.

'Breathe everybody,' she said. 'Deep breaths. Deeeeeep, slowwwww breaths. Let's do some lovely, relaxing visualization – close your eyes. All of you, darlings. Yes, even the Oranges. No talking. Close your eyes and imagine you're in a lovely meadow, the sun setting, the light like molten gold. Let that lovely golden light fill you up like a jar being filled with honey. That's it – some very good work from the Pinks over there – imagine everyone calming down at the end of a long, tiring day, the birds tucking themselves into their nests, the bees settling down in the hives, the rabbits—'

There was a burst of screaming.

'No rabbits,' said Ella, hastily. 'And there's a warm breeze stirring the golden grasses and you feel completely happy and unworried and ready to listen. And now . . . open your eyes.'

A hall full of calm Wimblies blinked back at her, and there was silence apart from a gentle snore from a collapsed Yellow.

'Right,' said Ella, modestly stepping back, 'I think Fidge can carry on now.'

'That was amazing,' said Graham, awestruck. 'Totally amazing.'

'And *that*,' said Dr Carrot, to Graham, 'was a very nice thing to say to someone.'

Graham looked embarrassed, but pleased.

'Someone else should tell them the plan,' said Fidge. 'I mucked it up the first time.'

Graham shook his head, still feeling rather warm inside. 'You'll be fine.'

Fidge gave him a narrow look; she wasn't quite sure if she believed in an amiable Graham. 'Let's do it together,' she suggested. 'You can start.'

# TWENTY-EIGHT

It was dawn, three hours later, with the sky just beginning to lighten and the first birds tentatively twittering. Fidge was standing on a hump-backed bridge overlooking the railway track and with her was a team of Greens, who claimed to have a foolproof plan for stopping the train. In the far distance they could just see the roof of the station, where Graham and Ella and the Oldest and Wisest of the Greys were waiting.

'It's coming,' said Fidge. From behind she could hear the approaching roar of the train, and she lifted her wrist and focused on her luminous watch dial. As the engine dived under the bridge, she started timing.

The train full of Greys disappeared into the distance, off on another circuit, the noise dwindled and for a minute or two there was nothing to hear but birdsong. Then faintly, from behind, the roar began again. As the engine neared, Fidge began to count aloud.

'Four minutes thirty-six, thirty-seven, thirty-eight, thirty-nine, *forty*.' The last four numbers of the count were almost drowned out by the thunder of the train passing beneath them once again.

One of the Greens stepped towards the parapet of the bridge, leaned over it for a long moment, staring at the track below, and then turned to Fidge.

'I'm going to jump onto the train
The next time it comes round again.
Once on the roof, I'll climb inside
And find the brake and stop the ride.
Can you count downwards, one by one
The last ten seconds of this run?
I'll make the leap when you reach "three"
And that should do it.
Hopefully.'

'Are you sure?' asked Fidge, keeping her eyes fixed on the watch, and making frantic mental calculations. 'It sounds unbelievably dangerous. Just over a minute left before it comes round again,' she added. Out of the corner of her eye, she could see the Green climbing onto the parapet, and positioning itself right on the edge.

'Fifty seconds to go,' said Fidge.

The Wimbley turned and spoke to the other Greens, who had clustered close by.

'If I don't make it, try once more
But next time make the jump at "four".
If that should fail, try "one" or "two"—'
'No, no,' shouted another of the Greens,
    'we want to jump with you!
For whether we leap at "ten" or "zero"
Let's die a team or live a hero!'

And the whole bunch of Greens started scrambling onto the narrow parapet, elbowing each other, fighting for space.

'Twenty seconds to go,' said Fidge. '*Please* be careful!'

The train noise was tremendous now, the bridge vibrating.

'Ten seconds,' shouted Fidge. 'Nine. Eight. Seven. Six. Five—'

With a great shout, one of the Greens overbalanced, grabbed onto the others, and the entire lot disappeared over the side. Fidge ran forward into a faceful of steam, and by the time it cleared she could just see the tail lights of the train snaking away into the distance.

'Hello?' she shouted. 'Anyone hurt?'

There was no reply.

The sun had edged over the horizon now, and in the greyish light, Fidge could spot the small anxious crowd on the station platform. The banners they'd brought with them were streaks of white in the gloom.

She crossed her fingers, and waited for the train to come back round. It seemed to take longer than before, but at last, the faint, familiar noise began again, except that this time there was another note to it, a hideous, high-pitched, grinding screech that grew shriller and louder and more and more unbearable until it sounded like someone pushing a giant fridge very slowly across a concrete floor.

*The brakes!* thought Fidge, stuffing her fingers into her ears. The train came gradually into view and as it passed beneath the bridge she could see Greens clinging onto the roof, and a green arm waving from the cab at the front. And as the train drew into the station, the wave turned into a triumphant thumbs-up.

Fidge ran.

By the time she got there, the platform was full of Greys, all of them looking rather dazed and wobbly, and all of them keen to stop and thank her, at tremendous length, for saving them from the train.

'I didn't do anything,' she kept saying, 'it was the Greens.' And as she spoke, she was helping Graham and Ella to unfurl the banners they'd made, and then to tie them along the side of the train. There was a banner for each of the six carriages, the messages written in huge letters:

**ALL WIMBLEY WOOS ARE INVITED TO
THE FIRST EVER SUGAR GAMES, STARTING
TODAY AT MIDDAY AT THE SPORTS FIELD.
SIX CHALLENGING COMPETITIONS,
SIX CHANCES TO WIN
ALL THE SWEETS YOU CAN EAT!!!**

'All right,' shouted Graham. 'They're secure!'

The Green in the engine cab gave a wave, there was a hiss and a great huff of steam, and the train pulled slowly out of the station.

Someone tugged at Fidge's sleeve, and she turned to see an anxious-looking Grey.

'This is no time for games and fun!
We need to summon everyone
For now that you have freed us all
It is imperative we call
A meeting where we'll give our views
On how we should confront the Blues.'

'We've already had a meeting,' said Fidge. 'The Games are part of the plan – it didn't take long to think it up. You see, the train's going to travel really slowly so that all the Blues on guard at the castle will see the banners and then they'll . . . What's the matter?' she asked; the Greys were all staring at her, shocked.

'But "thinking" is the job of *Greys*,' said one of them,
  voice squeaking with outrage.
'And planning should take several days.
Before we act, we really must
Make sure that everything's discussed.'


'But we don't *have* several days,' said Fidge. 'Not any more.
And the plan's already happening – all the other Wimblies have
worked right through the night preparing the sports field.'

'And you can't swan in and take over everything just
because you think you're clever,' added Graham.

'And, anyway, we *had* a Grey with us, the one who was
in jail,' said Fidge, pointing over at Ella and her companion.
'Let's hear what the Oldest and Wisest of you all has to say
about it.'

Ella leaned over and whispered in the ear of the Oldest
and Wisest – Fidge heard the word 'brief' – and it nodded,
and stepped up onto a luggage trolley, so as to be visible to
the crowd. There was a moment's silence, and then it spoke.

'I'm a fan
Of the plan
And so
Let's go.'


It climbed back down off the trolley, to total silence, apart
from a whoop and a high-five from Ella.

The other Greys looked as if they'd been hit with a sandbag. Fidge caught Graham's eye and snorted with laughter, before recovering herself.

'You heard what the Oldest and Wisest said,' she called. 'Let's go!'

# TWENTY-NINE

'**Y**ou've done an absolutely marvellous job,' said Ella, surveying the sports field. 'Well done everyone, splendid work.'

While Fidge and the others had been at the station, the rest of the Wimblies had finished preparing the competition area. On one side of the field was a large striped tent, labelled WINNERS! and decorated with balloons and hastily painted pictures of sweets. Silver streamers dangled over the entrance, so that nothing could be seen of the interior.

Next to it was a sad little roped-off patch of grass, labelled LOSERS' ENCLOSURE.

On the opposite side of the field, several rows of spectator benches were lined up and beside them was the Judge's Platform, dominated by a schedule board.

# SUGAR GAMES TIMETABLE.

1. Blindfold Obstacle Race
2. Cycling Relay
3. Dares
4. Charades
5. 100m Sprint
6. Swimming Race
7. Presentation of all remaining sweets to those who haven't won anything yet but who've waited quietly and without fuss in the losers' enclosure.

On the field, two identical obstacle-race courses had been set up next to each other. There were tunnels to climb through, hurdles to step over, bars to crawl under, bollards to weave around, bells to ring, balloons to burst and trays of glue to avoid. A group of Greens was warming up close by, swapping deafening fitness tips as they jogged in circles.

'So all we need now is for some Blues to arrive,' said Dr Carrot. 'I wonder if Graham's spotted any yet?'

Graham had startled everyone by offering to take first shift as look-out. 'I just want to help,' he'd said modestly, but the real reason was a sudden longing for some time on his own. He wasn't used to being part of a crowd, and though all the praise he'd been getting was very pleasant – and, of course, totally deserved – the effort of being nicer than usual was beginning to exhaust him. And now that he'd climbed what felt like a thousand steps to the terrace at the top of the king's column in the Town Square, he was feeling even more exhausted. He rested his elbows on the railing and trained his binoculars on the castle. It was immediately obvious that something was going on: clusters of Blues were standing on the steep slopes of the castle mound, looking towards where the railway track passed closest to the moat. After a minute or two, the train puffed slowly into view, banners rippling in the wind. The Blues pointed excitedly and a small group broke away from the others and set off towards the bridge. Graham waited until they were safely across the moat and heading towards Wimbley Town before he took a piece of paper and scribbled:

### 6 BLUES ON THEIR WAY TO YOU FROM THE CASTLE

He wrapped the paper round a small stone.

'Hey,' he shouted, over the railing, 'I've got a message for Fidge.'

A Yellow, stationed underneath, waved and stepped back as Graham dropped the stone. Catching it neatly, it mounted a taxi-bike and sped off.

Graham checked the castle again and saw the great door swing open as another group of Blues came out. In the moment before it shut again, he glimpsed the interior, and frowned. What he'd expected to see was the courtyard. What he actually saw was a colour: a deep, velvety red – shapeless and sinister.

Uneasily, he swung the binoculars round to look at the countryside and his heart skipped with fear. Wimbley Land was disappearing so fast, the border was now no more than a mile away from where he stood; beyond it was a world like a blank page.

The train was shunting round again and Blues were starting to stream over the moat and towards the town, dozens of them.

Graham scribbled another note, and waited for the taxi-cyclist to return. In the distance, he could see the first Blues arriving at the sports field.

'Welcome,' said Dr Carrot, to the teams assembled for the first race. 'I shall be setting out the rules for each of the competitions. We have two teams of six lining up here for the obstacle race. Five members of each team will be blindfolded, and the sixth member will be responsible for calling out the instructions. Competitors go one at a time along the course. First team to get all five blindfolded members safely home, wins. To avoid confusion, the teams will start from *opposite* ends of the course. Any questions? No? Good. Before we start, our judge would like to give a speech.'

There was a stifled groan of boredom from one of the Wimblies. The Oldest and Wisest of the Greys stepped forward. It gazed solemnly at the six Blues and the six Greens, and then spoke.

'Fair play.
OK?'

It stepped back.
'Thank you,' said Dr Carrot. 'So let's begin.'

Fidge, meanwhile, was in the Winners' Tent. Nobody had won anything yet, but it was the only place where she could have a private chat with a crowd of panicking Yellows.

'You're not *fighting* the Blues, you're just going to race them,' she said, for what felt like the hundredth time. 'You're great at cycling, you'll easily beat them.'

One of the Yellows raised a hand, and spoke tremulously:

'But we don't want to beat the Blues
We'd feel much safer if we lose.'

There was mass nodding.

'But you *can't* lose,' said Fidge, her voice cracking with desperation. 'If you lose, then the Blues will realize that there are no sweets for the winners and then the whole plan's ruined. We *have* to keep them shut up in the Losers' Enclosure. It's not hard, all you have to do is pedal!'

'No,' said Ella, from behind her. 'All they have to do is *believe* in themselves. I think I should conduct a little workshop.' She raised her voice. 'Everyone find a nice spot and lie down – anywhere will do, you don't have to be next to your friends. Ready? All right, now I want you to close your eyes and repeat after me: "I am Yellow. I am Mighty".'

There was a pause.

'They can't say it unless it rhymes,' whispered Fidge.

'Repeat after me,' said Ella, not missing a beat. 'I am Yellow. I am Mighty, I am brave and never Frighty.'

'I didn't think "Frighty" was a word,' said Fidge.

'Perhaps you'd like to go and see how the others are getting on,' suggested Ella, with a slight edge to her voice. 'Give me ten minutes.'

Fidge went outside and sat on a spectator bench, and then stood up again and paced around. The obstacle race was just about to begin, and she felt hugely nervous; it would be the first test of their plan.

'On your marks,' called Dr Carrot.

The Greens were lined up at one end of the field, the first blindfolded team member standing just in front of their first obstacle, a narrow crawl-through tunnel.

At the opposite end of the field, a line of blindfolded Blues was standing in front of *their* first obstacle, a series of glue-filled trays.

'Get set.'

The competitors tensed themselves. The Wimblies who were going to be shouting the instructions each took a deep breath.

'Go!'

'First you must—' began the Blue instructor, before being totally and completely drowned out by the Green bellowing from the other end of the field:

'Now listen! Quickly, first of all
Lie down upon the ground and crawl.'

'Brilliant!' said Fidge, as the blindfolded Blue obediently lay down full length in a tray of glue. The blindfolded Green sped through the tunnel and arrived at a balloon pit.

'Don't—' began the Blue instructor.

'Balloons are lying on the ground
So now stand up and jump around.'

The Green competitor started bursting the balloons, quickly and efficiently, while at the other end of the field there was utter chaos, the blindfolded Blue staggering around with a tray stuck to its front and another one on each foot. It tripped on the next obstacle, a bollard, and fell over, thrashing feebly.

Fidge was applauding when she felt someone brush past her, and she turned to see a trickle of spectators making their way to the benches. She stared at them – a pale Orange, a bleached Green, a trio of pallid Purples. They sat in a line, their arms folded, their expressions listless.

'These benches are a bit hard,' said a pallid Purple.

'Yes,' said the pale Orange.

On the field, the third member of the Green team had just completed the obstacle course, while the first member of the Blue team was still wandering hopelessly in the wrong direction, a bollard glued to its backside.

'Good job, Greens!' shouted Fidge, applauding. 'You're doing brilliantly, keep going!'

She glanced over at the silent spectators, sitting there like a row of mugs on a shelf, and she felt a painful twist of fear; if the plan failed, then *this* was the future for herself, for Graham, for all of them. There would be no going home – *ever*. She sprinted towards the tent to find out how Ella was getting on, and then stepped hastily aside as a double row of Yellows jogged out. They were chanting in unison, their voices loud and confident:

'We are Yellows, we are tough
No one else is good enough.
We've got on our cycling shoes
Gonna beat those no-good Blues!'

'Remember,' called Ella, 'think *inner* strength.' She aimed a high-five at Fidge, and then pointed with her trunk towards the edge of the field, where the bike-messenger had just pedalled up; it was holding out another note from Graham.

Ella waited while Fidge hurried to collect it.

'What's it say, darling?'

Fidge read the note and swallowed.

'It says,' she said, 'that we're running out of time.'

# THIRTY

From his watchtower, Graham could see the Losers' Enclosure beginning to fill. The team of Blues who'd lost the obstacle race had been joined by the team of Blues who'd been lapped three times in the cycling relay and the team of Blues who'd failed to win a single point in a game of charades against the Purples, as well as the team of Blues who'd been beaten so badly at dares by the Pinks that two of them had actually started crying. On the field, the Oranges were limbering up for the sprint; nearby, Fidge was fiddling with something on her arm.

Graham trained his binoculars on the castle again; the door had been left open and it gaped like a mouth awaiting food. He looked around for Blues, and for a second his spirits rose – there were none, the hillside was empty at last, the castle unguarded! But then he saw that the guards on the moat bridge were still there. They all had red berets and they stood, steadfast and immoveable, ignoring the banners on the train as it steamed by for the umpteenth time. It was clear that these were the most loyal of the Blues and they were not going to leave their post; the moat would have to be crossed some other way.

Graham lowered the binoculars, thinking hard, an idea beginning to sprout.

He wrote a quick note and peered over the railing to look for the messenger Yellow. There was no sign of the taxi-bike in the square below him, nor over at the sports field. It wasn't until his eye followed the wiggling road between the two places that he saw what had happened: one of the curves in the lane had taken the bike over the white border – now so horribly near – and it was parked there, its colourless rider sitting in the saddle, feet dangling aimlessly. It didn't even turn its head when Graham shouted.

'On your marks,' called Dr Carrot, by the sprint track. The Blues crouched at their blocks, determination visible in every feature. The Oranges shuffled around in a giggling group fairly near the start line.

'Get set,' called Dr Carrot.

'Hey,' said Fidge, walking over to the Oranges. 'Look at this, I had a bit of an accident, it's quite bad.' She held out her arm. It was loosely wrapped in a bandage on which she'd smudged some red paint. The Oranges stopped giggling. Fidge started to untie it. The Oranges edged away.

'Go!' called Dr Carrot.

Fidge ripped off the bandage and the Oranges sprang away from her as if fired from a cannon. They caught up with the Blues halfway up the course, overtook them easily and carried on running even after they'd won by twenty metres.

'Sorry!' shouted Fidge, as the orange blurs disappeared into the far distance. 'I'm really sorry, but it had to be done.'

The defeated team trudged, drooping with failure, into the Losers' Enclosure, which was now completely packed with depressed-looking Blues.

'Could all competitors for the final race, assemble at the swimming pool,' announced Dr Carrot.

Fidge turned to follow the remaining handful of Blues, and then swung back to look at something – a figure coming towards her across the field. It was Graham. It was Graham, *running*.

She hurried to meet him.

'I . . . ha . . . huh . . . di . . . wa . . .' said Graham, struggling to breathe, his face bright pink. He leaned over with his hands on his knees. 'Muh . . . moh . . . bluh . . . swi . . .'

He mimed swimming. 'Swi . . .'

'What's the matter?' asked Fidge, scanning the field behind him. 'Is someone chasing you?'

Graham shook his head. 'No . . .' he gasped. 'It's just . . .

I've never . . . I've never . . .' He took a huge, deep breath and then gabbled the next few words, 'neverrunanywherebefore.' He lowered himself to the ground, and lay there, panting.

Ella breezed across. 'Try not to speak for a while, darling,' she said. '*Mime* your message, and I'll interpret.' She watched Graham intently, as he waved his arms. 'You've seen a kite. Someone's flying a kite above the castle – no, not a kite, a hot-air balloon. With a fish on it. A fish and a banana.'

'*No.*' Graham struggled upright. 'We've got to hurry . . . all the Blues have gone . . . except for the guards with the berets on the bridge and I don't think they're going to move . . . but I've thought of another way to cross the moat . . . we could . . . we could . . .' He ran out of breath again, and gestured vaguely.

'Build a bridge,' said Ella, concentrating hard. 'Build a bridge for us all to cross out of something that makes you go to sleep. Out of pillows?'

'Not pillows,' said Fidge, suddenly understanding. 'Out of *Greys*. I get it – I get it!'

Graham nodded, relieved, and Fidge was off, running towards Dr Carrot, then towards the swimming pool, where the competitors were waiting for the final race.

'Change of plan!' she shouted, as she went along. 'The final race is taking place at the moat, instructions when we get there. Follow me! Quickly, everyone, quickly!'

'Do you know something?' said Ella, to Graham, as she helped him up. 'I think that you two make rather a good team.'

'This should do it,' whispered Fidge to Dr Carrot. She had led the two teams – Blues and Greys – right round the back of the castle, so that the hillside blocked them from the view of the guards on the bridge. They were now assembled beside the moat, together with Ella and Graham (still slightly pink in the face) and the Oldest and Wisest of the Greys.

Dr Carrot turned squeakily to address the crowd. The hurried journey from the sports field seemed to have damaged something on her wheelbase, so that she was on a severe slant. She spoke rapidly.

'This is the final competition of the day, and so we've decided to create a really difficult challenge. Your task is to make a floating bridge going from one side of the moat to the other, and for one of your team to cross it safely. Speed is of the essence. If it's complete in under five minutes, there will be extra prizes! Would our judge like to say anything?'

'No,' said the Grey. *'Go!'*

The Wimblies stormed into the water, the Blues swimming in a splashy, show-off style and the Greys doing a kind of dignified doggy paddle. Fidge noticed that they floated far higher in the water than their rivals.

'Come on!' she shouted, jigging up and down with tension. The Blues were halfway across the moat now, their thrashing arms throwing up great sheets of reddish water.

*Reddish?*

Fidge frowned and then knelt to scoop up a handful;

in her palm it looked normal.

'The colour's a reflection,' said Graham, who'd been watching her. 'Look at the castle.'

She looked up and saw the crimson of the doorway, so deep and dark that it seemed to stain the air around it.

There was a shout from the far shore of the moat as the first Blue touched land.

'Remember,' shouted Dr Carrot, 'it's not just a speed race, it's a structural challenge. We need a functional bridge, capable of holding a *considerable* load.'

'Tiny bit personal, darling,' murmured Ella.

The next Blue to reach the bank grabbed the feet of the first, the Blue after that hung onto the heels of the second and amazingly quickly, a chain of Wimblies was formed, stretching unbroken across the water. The single guard remaining on the bank raised its arms in triumph.

'The Greys are beaten fair and square
We've won this race, we want our share
And now these games have been contested
You strangers must be re-arrested.'

'No,' said Dr Carrot, calmly and swiftly. 'The rule is that one member of your team has to cross over the bridge to the other side.'

The Blue looked annoyed, but stepped off the bank onto the stomach of the first link of the chain. It sank immediately.

The Blue stumbled forward onto the second link, which also sank, and then fell full-length onto the third. This time both of them sank. Within seconds, the moat was full of coughing, thrashing Blues, the chain irreparably broken.

'And now you have to start all over again,' said Dr Carrot. 'Remember, if you're defeated you need to join your colleagues in the Losers' Enclosure to have *any chance* of leftover sweets.'

'Look at the other team!' called Ella, admiringly.

The Grey bridge was almost complete, the Wimblies floating high in the water, their grip on each other steady and secure. Their team leader stepped forward.

'Before I cross, I want to say
That it has—'

'Sorry, no time!' shouted Fidge, pushing past. She and Graham lifted Dr Carrot and started unsteadily across the bridge, struggling to balance on the curved, bobbing surfaces. Fidge was concentrating so hard, that she was two-thirds across before she realized that Dr Carrot was speaking.

'What did you say?' she asked.

'You need to go faster.'

'What? Why?' She glanced behind her.

The Oldest and Wisest of the Greys was stepping cautiously onto the bridge and Ella was still on the bank, waiting her turn. And just a yard or two beyond Ella, the world was as white as a frosted cake.

# THIRTY-ONE

'**W**hat are you *doing*?' shouted Graham, as Fidge doubled her speed across the bridge, teetering from one Wimbley to the next.

'Just keep up!' she shouted back. They reached the far side of the moat in a stumbling rush, falling into a heap on the grass.

'Had to,' said Fidge, between gasps. 'Just look!'

The Oldest and Wisest was halfway across, but Ella had only just stepped onto the Wimbley bridge. She walked delicately (for an elephant) but even so, the first Grey sank slowly beneath her weight, only springing to the surface again once she'd inched carefully onto the second.

'Come on!!' called Fidge, in an agony of tension. The whiteness had reached the very edge of the moat and was beginning to creep across the water. Several of the Blues had clambered out, seemingly with the intention of stopping Ella, but they were now standing on the bank, colourless hands on faded hips, talking about lawnmower repairs.

Ella extended a tentative foot towards the third link of the bridge.

'She'll have to swim,' muttered Graham.

'You'll have to swim!' shouted Fidge.

'No, darling, it's not one of my skills.'

'I bet it is,' said Graham. 'I've seen documentaries about swimming elephants.'

'Just do it!' yelled Fidge. 'Hurry!!!'

'They're right,' said Dr Carrot. 'I'm usually an advocate of free choice but this time you have run out of options. Now JUMP!!!'

The unexpectedly loud order seemed to startle Ella. She mis-timed her next step, started to topple, and attempted to turn the fall into a graceful dive. She hit the moat with a noise like a gas explosion. A great sheet of water rose up and then splattered down, as if a sudden rainstorm had begun. And when it cleared, there was Ella, powering through the water like a speedboat, trunk raised triumphantly.

She reached the bank at the same time as the Oldest and Wisest, and climbed out, laughing girlishly, water cascading from her hair. The five of them started up the steep slope towards the castle. Within seconds there was a loud snap and Dr Carrot keeled over sideways.

'Leave me,' she ordered. 'My axle's gone.'

'Don't be ridiculous,' said Fidge, 'we're not leaving anyone behind.' She and Graham hoisted the carrot between them again and tried to hurry up the slope, but the grass was rough and Graham kept stumbling with exhaustion, his face pale and sweaty.

'Not too far now,' said Ella. 'Let's imagine we're butterflies, dancing effortlessly in mid-air.'

'I'm actually just about to throw up,' said Graham.

'Now we can stop,' called the Oldest and Wisest, from the front.

'We've reached the top.'

Fidge lifted her gaze from her feet, and saw the stern and windowless sweep of the castle wall. Craning her head right back, she could just see the battlements, and above them, a row of flags and two dark red banners, sticking up at odd angles.

'I would suggest,' said Dr Carrot, from her horizontal position, 'that we take a minute to compose ourselves, before continuing round the base to the door.'

Panting, Fidge leaned against the wall, and turned to see the view.

The old Wimbley Land, in all its harlequin splendour, had gone. In its place was a scene from an unused colouring book: trees the same shade as train tracks and lakes as pale as hedges. And as her breathing quietened, Fidge realized something else: Wimbley Land was deathly quiet. There was no birdsong, no chatter, no shouting guards, no tinkle of bicycle bells, no splash of fountains, no shiver of wind in the trees.

The only colour, and the only source of any sound, was the top half of the hill on which they were standing.

'Darlings,' said Ella, and her voice was trembling, 'let's go now and sort this out.'

In silence and in single file – a scared, tired, determined little army – they trudged round the base of the castle. And then stopped.

The double doors stood open, but a huge dark-red object, the size of a van, was sticking out through them.

'What's *that*?' Asked Graham, in a whisper.

They edged closer.

The huge dark-red object had a pinkish square, like a ragged tablecloth, flopping down from it. And scattered across the pinkish square were odd black marks.

'I think that's writing,' hissed Fidge. 'Maybe it's a message.'

She set down Dr Carrot, and tiptoed forward, tilting her head to try and read what was written.

'I can see "DO NOT",' she whispered over her shoulder, 'and there's a picture of a sort of pan thing with a cross through it. "DO NOT . . . BOIL. DO NOT TUMBLE DRY. USE COLD WATER AND MILD DETERGENTS ONLY".'

There was a pause.

'Somewhat puzzling,' said Dr Carrot.

Fidge backed away and shook her head. 'It's not puzzling at all,' she said, hoarsely. 'It's the washing instructions label on Wed Wabbit's foot.'

'His *foot*?' repeated Graham. 'If that's his foot, then what's the rest of him like?'

They all stared at the van-sized object, and then Ella reached out her trunk and gave it a tiny poke.

# 'GUARDS!!'

Ella leaped back; it was Wed Wabbit's voice and it wasn't so much loud, as *everywhere*, so that Fidge felt her whole body vibrate with the word.

# 'GUARDS!! I WEQUIWE YOUR PWESENCE! WE HAVE INTWUDERS ATTEMPTING TO BWEAK INTO THE FORTWESS.'

The shriek of rage died away, till all Fidge could hear

was the thudding of her own heart. Nothing moved on the hilltop, apart from the steady onward creep of the white line.

'But there are no guards,' said Dr Carrot, quietly. 'Not any more.'

'That's true,' said Fidge. She walked up to the doors and saw that there was a gap between Wed Wabbit's foot and the frame.

'We can get through here,' she said. 'He might be big, but there's only one of him and there's five of us.'

'But that's meaningless,' said Graham. 'That's like saying five ants can defeat an *anteater*.' He glanced back at the sterile land and wondered whether it would be better to stay outside, to become one of those bored and boring shadows, discussing shoe polish and the hardness of seats, or whether he should follow his mad cousin, who was currently helping Ella to squeeze through the gap.

'What if I die?' he said, out loud.

'What if you live?' countered Dr Carrot, irritatingly.

Graham felt a shove, and turned to see the Oldest and Wisest, standing just behind him.

'Are you *pushing* me?' he asked, incredulously.

The Grey nodded.

'Too late
For debate.
Don't talk.
Just walk.'

'He's right,' said Fidge, returning to pick up Dr Carrot. 'Come *on.*'

Reluctantly, fearfully, Graham followed.

# THIRTY-TWO

'**GUARDS!!**' shrieked Wed Wabbit as, one by one, Fidge and her companions emerged round his gigantic foot into the roofless courtyard.

'AWWEST THESE WEBELS. AWWEST THEM STWAIGHT AWAY! GUARDS!!! WHY ARE YOU NOT WESPONDING TO MY ORDERS? THERE

# WILL BE NO WEWARDS UNLESS YOU WESPOND.'

The echoes of his voice slammed from wall to wall. Fidge stuffed her fingers in her ears, and gazed upward.

Since her last view of him, Wed Wabbit had quadrupled in size, his great round body nearly filling the space, his arms wedged against the walls, his head silhouetted against the sky. And she realized, with a jolt, that those oddly angled red banners that she'd seen from the moat weren't banners at all – they were Wed Wabbit's ears, poking high above the battlements.

'Can we talk to you?' shouted Fidge.

# 'GUARDS!'

'There aren't any guards.'

# 'WHERE ARE MY GUARDS?'

'Can you just listen for half a second? There aren't any—'

# 'I WANT MY GUARDS!!!'

shouted Wed Wabbit again, and he seemed to expand even more, the fury in his voice shaking the walls and sending little puffs of mortar trickling down into the courtyard.

'Did you see that?' squeaked Graham. 'He just *got even bigger*! If we go outside we'll get bleached and if we stay in here we'll get crushed.'

One of the van-sized feet stamped petulantly and the whole castle shook; it stamped again and one of the throne-room doors fell off, breaking in half as it hit the floor.

For a split-second, Fidge was reminded of the time when Minnie, aged two, had had a tantrum in a supermarket and her kicking foot had knocked over a vast pyramid of fruit, sending oranges rolling as far as the car park. '*Have a little word with Wed Wabbit,*' Minnie had said on the phone, but you couldn't ever talk to someone who was having a tantrum; you just had to sit it out and wait for them to calm down.

# 'GUARDS!!'

Fidge put her hands in her pockets and leaned back against the wall. 'Ignore him,' she hissed to the others. 'Totally ignore him.'

'Are you mad?' asked Graham, ducking as a chunk of plaster skittered to the floor.

'No, completely serious. It's our only chance.'

# 'WHY ARE YOU DISOBEYING ME?'

One of the vast arms swung and part of the battlement fell off; Fidge could hear stones thudding to the ground outside. There was a brief pause. Ella carefully and deliberately brushed a speck of dust from her cardigan.

# 'THESE INTWUDERS MUST LEAVE

# OR THERE WILL BE TWOUBLE!!'

The Grey gave a little yawn.

# 'TEWWIBLE TEWWIBLE TWOUBLE!!'

Graham, though looking sick with terror, managed to whistle a feeble tune. Dr Carrot actually appeared to be asleep.

There was a longer pause. Fidge was avoiding looking directly at Wed Wabbit, but out of the corner of her eye, she could see his head swivel as he looked along the line of intruders. One of his ears caught on a flag. The pole snapped and the rectangle of red silk fluttered slowly down into the courtyard.

# 'MY GUARDS WILL BE HERE VEWY SOON!'

shouted Wed Wabbit again, but there was a doubtful note in his voice.

This time, the silence was really long.

'Can I say something now?' Asked Fidge.

# 'NO. GO AWAY.'

Wed Wabbit raised a threatening foot.

'It's your own castle you're destroying,' said Dr Carrot.

Wed Wabbit lowered his foot again.

'We need a little talk,' said Fidge.

# 'I DON'T WANT TO TALK.'

'Well in that case, you just need to *listen*.'

# 'GUARDS!'

'There are no guards,' said Fidge, 'because you've sucked all the colour and life out of Wimbley Land! Have you even looked out of the castle?'

# 'YOU CANNOT

# QUESTION ME. I AM IN CHARGE HERE.'

'In charge of what?' asked Graham. 'There's nothing left to be in charge *of*. You had a whole country of your own and you ruined it.'

'By behaving like a bully,' said Dr Carrot.

'And I don't think it's made you awfully happy, has it?' Asked Ella. 'Because being in charge isn't at all the same as being popular.'

The rabbit seemed to quiver slightly, and his head swivelled away from Ella, as if he could no longer bear to meet her gaze.

'And I bet you're lonely,' added Graham, more quietly. 'I bet you're really, really lonely. No one likes you and you're trying to pretend you don't mind, but I bet you're actually feeling horrible.'

Wed Wabbit's head was silhouetted so it was hard to see his expression, but he gave a furious little hunch of the shoulders, dislodging another shower of plaster.

'Except Minnie,' said Fidge, looking up at him. 'Minnie *loves* you and she's missing you desperately. And I bet you're missing her too.'

For a moment nothing happened, and then Wed Wabbit's ears drooped and he slumped forward, his head thudding against the wall, high above Fidge. A crack shot up from the foundations to the battlements, like a zip being opened; a torrent of stones rattled down and then, with a noise like thunder, a huge chunk of wall collapsed outward, revealing a section of whitened hillside.

'I think someone's feeling a little bit sad,' whispered Ella.

Wed Wabbit slumped still further, his face squashed against the wall, his arms dangling hopelessly. More cracks appeared in the stonework.

Fidge raised her voice. 'So I want you to have a good think about your behaviour,' she said, kindly but firmly, and the words and their tone were so familiar to her that she could almost hear her mother's voice saying them. 'And then you need to work out how you can make things all better again.'

There was a long pause and then Wed Wabbit shrugged. Another bit of wall fell over and through the gap, the whiteness crept onward into the castle.

Fidge looked helplessly at Ella. 'What now?' she whispered. 'I've said all the things my mum usually says.'

'Are you sure of that, darling?' asked Ella. 'Are you absolutely certain?'

'Yes I . . .' Fidge hesitated. 'Oh.' She clenched her fists and then unclenched them.

*'And finally, just one of you, Must find the hardest thing to do,'* quoted Ella, gently.

'Come on, come on,' urged Graham. 'Whatever it is, just do it, or we're all doomed. You're always doing brave stuff, what's the problem now? Get *on* with it.' He ducked as another avalanche of plaster cascaded down the wall.

'I think you'll find,' said Dr Carrot, 'that bravery comes in many forms.'

Fidge walked forward until she was right next to Wed Wabbit, directly beneath his drooping head, and then she spoke. 'My sister Minnie said that when I found you, I had to give you something. And now I know what that something is.' She took a deep, deep breath. 'Want a hug?' she asked.

Ten seconds went by. Then another ten. And then Wed Wabbit moved his head very slightly in a tiny, almost imperceptible nod.

Stiffly, Fidge opened her arms and embraced as much of him as she could reach.

It was a long time since she'd given anyone a hug. Two and a half years, to be precise. She thought of her dad, so bulky in his fireman's uniform that she hadn't been able to get her arms all the way round him. 'Fidge the Mighty', her dad had called her, 'Strong Girl'.

She hugged tighter, the red velvet squashy beneath her cheek, her eyes shut, the muscles in her arms beginning to ache. She hung on, her mind a blank. Time stopped.

And then the world turned upside down.

# THIRTY-THREE

She was tumbling through the air, whirled by a hot wind, her ears blatting and popping with sudden pressure, her vision striped and blurred.

'Fidge!'

She was lying on her back, her head pounding.

'Fidge, are you OK?' She opened her eyes and saw a cloudless blue sky, and then Graham's worried face.

'Yes, I'm OK,' she said, automatically. She raised a hand and rubbed her forehead and felt a small object roll beneath her fingers. She picked it up and held it in front of her eyes. It was a jelly bean.

'You did it,' said Graham.

'Did what?'

Ella loomed into view. 'It's a triumph!' she exclaimed. 'An absolute triumph!'

'Well done.

We've won!' called the Oldest and Wisest, from somewhere behind her.

Fidge struggled up onto her elbow and flinched at the brilliance of the view. The castle was completely flattened, the walls knocked outward, as if by a gigantic explosion. And Wimbley Land was back, blazing with colour, bursting with sound, birds singing, wind ruffling the hillside grasses and swaying the treetops. In fact, if anything, it looked even *more* colourful than before, with orange and yellow blossoms blazing on all the trees, and red-and-purple birds swooping above the rubble. And there were sweets everywhere, dotting the grass like wildflowers.

'Good work,' said Dr Carrot, who was propped up against the splintered remains of the Rewards Room door, a tangle of strawberry licorice laces wrapped around her stem.

'But what happened?' asked Fidge, looking round, relief seeping into her bones like sunshine. She felt oddly light, as if she'd been carrying round a sack of stones, and had just put it down.

'One second Wed Wabbit was there,' said Graham, 'and the next he wasn't and it was like a paintbox blowing up or a really huge kaleidoscope falling to bits or being shut inside a washing machine filled with sweets or spun about by a tornado full of confetti or . . .' He shook his head, unable to describe it adequately.

'It was like the rainbow of peace that comes after the storm of rage,' said Ella.

Graham rolled his eyes at Fidge. '*No it wasn't,*' he mouthed.

'So where's Wed Wabbit now?' Asked Fidge, looking around. Her gaze snagged an object lying just within her reach. It was a red velvet rabbit, slightly dusty and just over a foot long. She reached out and grabbed it by the ears.

'Oh *no,*' said Graham.

'What?'

'The Blues are coming back.'

A cluster of guards was marching up the hill towards them. Hastily, Fidge tucked Wed Wabbit under one arm and clambered to her feet, bracing herself for yet another struggle.

One of the Blues gave a little wave and then bent to pick up a sweet.

'It waved,' muttered Graham, out of the side of his mouth.

Another of the Blues stumbled slightly, and then started giggling.

'Are they *drunk*?' asked Graham.

'I don't know,' said Fidge, squinting into the sunlight, 'but they look incredibly odd.'

The solid, deep colour of each Blue was now randomly spotted and streaked. The giggler was splashed with orange and the one who'd waved at Graham had a smudge of pink across its front. One of the other Blues seemed to have been partially dipped in purple; it was doing a little dance and had made itself a crown of woven grass.

'The explosion's mixed everything up,' said Fidge.

She could see other Wimblies making their way up towards the castle: a Green with yellow feet was sharing a bar of chocolate with a giggling Grey whose arms were covered in orange polka dots; two blue-dappled Yellows were jogging shoulder to shoulder and exchanging vigorous remarks.

'A whole new society!' exclaimed Ella, stepping forward to greet one of the spotted Blues.

It spoke, its voice the usual rough gurgle:

'Accept our thanks for everything.
We've come to free our captured king
Restore him to his usual state
And afterwards invite everyone to a really enormous
    party going on until all hours with mountains of
    food and drink and sweets to celebrate.'

It hurried off towards the gaping hole that had once been the door to the dungeons, just as a Pink with blue-and-grey streaks and an enormous grin, strode up and gave Fidge a rib-crushing hug. Despite its coloration, it looked oddly familiar and she felt a shock of recognition.

'It's *you!*' she exclaimed, grinning back. 'I kept thinking about you, still stuck at the fairground. I never thanked you for everything – you were brilliant.'

'But it's us who can't thank *you* enough,' said the Pink, in serious, confident tones.
'We know that your journey's been rough.
For such a brave fight
Your talents were right
You're clever and stubborn and tough.'

'It wasn't just me,' said Fidge.

A Purple with green blotches clapped Graham on the back.

'One straw is so weak,' it bellowed.
'But take and weave a handful –
Such strength together!'

'That didn't rhyme,' said Fidge.

'Blank verse,' said Ella. 'Freedom of expression is blowing like a fresh breeze through Wimbley Land – can't you feel it? There's such artistic potential here! It's almost a pity that we have to go.'

'Go?' repeated Fidge. 'How? What do you mean?'

'The transport's here, darling – didn't you see it? It's down by the bridge.'

Suddenly breathless, Fidge turned to look.

Parked by the side of the moat was an enormous silver

bus with pink wheels, the sort of thing that an international film star might travel in, except that printed on the side, in letters large enough to read from the top of the hill, were the words:

## tHIS BELONGS to MINNIE HARKER

She turned to Graham. 'We can go home!' she said.

'Oh.' He paused. 'Good.'

'Aren't you pleased?'

'Yes, *of course* I am,' he said, irritably, turning away so that she couldn't see his expression. The word 'home' had filled him with a sudden, stifling sense of panic. In his mind's eye he could see drawn curtains and closed doors and the tired, worried faces of his parents.

He mooched over towards Dr Carrot, who was having her axle fixed by a Green-with-blue-splodges.

'Is something the matter?' she asked.

He shrugged, and kicked a cluster of gobstoppers across the flowered turf.

'You're my transitional object,' he said. 'That means you're supposed to help me cope with changes.'

'That's right.'

'But what if I *want* changes? What if I want things to be different at home? I'm sick of being scared of stairs and bikes and darkness. And small spaces and germs and being on my own and fires and cold water and going outside and hailstones and ants and thunder and those disgusting grey bits you sometimes find in fish fingers . . .'

Dr Carrot gave a little experimental roll back and forth. 'Much better,' she said to the Wimbley. 'I'm very grateful.'

'Are you listening?' asked Graham.

'I am both listening and being polite,' said Dr Carrot. 'It's quite possible to do both things simultaneously.'

'OK,' muttered Graham. 'Sorry.'

Dr Carrot's expression softened. 'In answer to your question – and it's a very fair one – if it's changes you're after, I can think of something that might be far more useful to you than a transitional object. More useful and also more enjoyable.'

'What?' asked Graham.

'A friend.'

'But how do I get one of those?'

Dr Carrot's gaze slid past him, towards Fidge. 'I think,' she said, 'you might almost already have one.'

There was a sudden commotion, and Graham turned to see the sludge-coloured figure of the king being hoisted shoulder-height by his rescuers. Yet more Wimblies – striped, streaked, spotted, dip-dyed, blotched and stippled – were streaming up the hillside, and crowding into the ruins of the castle.

'Speech!' called Ella. 'Remember, deep breath and then *project*.'

'Dear friends and subjects, thank you all,' said the king,
'For freeing me from the tyrant's thrall
But being shut up in a dungeon
Gave me time to think. Bim Bungeon.
And I've realized – don't be cross –
That I don't want to be your boss.
I much prefer to sit and chat
And therefore I've decided that
I'm going to abdicate and hope
You'll find a better king. Bip Bope.'

There was a buzz of shock and concern from the crowd.
The king raised his voice.

'My personal suggestion is
The Oldest, Wisest Grey. Fip fizz.'

Relieved cheering broke out and then the Wimblies who'd
hoisted the king above the crowd, hastily lowered him again
and picked up the Oldest and Wisest instead. The Grey held
up its hand for silence.

'One is wise, but two are wiser
I would like a good adviser.
Dr Carrot, could I ask
You stay and help me with this task?'

Everyone looked at Dr Carrot and Dr Carrot looked at Graham.

'It all depends on whether or not I can move on from my current job,' she said. 'Are you still in need of a transitional object?'

And now everyone looked at Graham.

He took a deep breath. 'No,' he said, trying to keep his voice firm, 'I think I'll try and manage without one.'

And the thin, straight black line that was Dr Carrot's mouth, curled suddenly upwards at the ends. It was nearly – *nearly* – a grin.

The Oldest and Wisest spoke again.

'And in this land of fresh new starts
We'll need a Minister for the Arts
And therefore I would like to know
If Ella—'

'Yes!!!!' screamed Ella, flinging up her trunk and both forelegs. 'Oh, darlings, it will be my pleasure. I've already had the most *marvellous* idea for a summer evening spectacular, starting with a dance sequence in and out of the ruins, followed by a mime in which we all symbolically re-build the castle. We can start work-shopping tomorrow.'

There was a chorus of whoops and cheers from the Wimblies, and Ella was lost in a swirl of colour.

Graham felt a touch on his shoulder.

'You coming?' asked Fidge. 'I think it's just the two of us now.'

He nodded, and they set off down the hill together.

'Though there are three of us, really,' added Fidge. She dusted off Wed Wabbit and took a look at him. His ears were bent and one of his eyes had worked loose, and instead of looking smugly superior, he looked harmless and slightly silly. She wondered why she'd ever hated him so much.

'Will your sister mind about not getting Ella back?' Asked Graham.

Fidge shook her head. 'She's got hundreds of other soft toys and I think the Wimblies need Ella more than Minnie does. What about you – do you mind losing Dr Carrot?'

'A bit. But back home she's not a doctor, is she? She's just a very small plastic toy I got free from the supermarket.' He glanced at Fidge. 'You always thought I was completely useless, didn't you?'

Fidge hesitated and then nodded. 'But you haven't been completely useless here,' she said. 'You've been helpful. And brave.'

'Thanks. And I always thought you were incredibly boring and stupid.'

'*Incredibly boring and stupid?*' repeated Fidge, outraged.

'But you're not.'

'I know!'

'In fact you're really quite clever.'

Fidge rolled her eyes. 'Thanks.'

'I'm just trying to be honest. Hang on,' he added. 'What on earth is *that*?' He was pointing towards the silver bus.

'What do you mean?'

'That thing. That black-and-white thing behind the steering wheel.'

'Oh that.' Fidge grinned. 'Minnie decided that the bus needed a driver so she wedged in a wind-up bath toy.'

'It's a whale.'

'Yes.'

'A killer whale.'

'Yes.'

There was a pause. 'Well,' said Graham, 'I hope it's passed its *diving* test.'

Fidge snorted. 'That's quite funny.'

From behind them came another cheer, and they turned to look back. The early evening sky was a delicate violet, and a huge moon was rising behind Wimbley Hill. Silhouetted against it was a conga line of Wimblies, headed by Ella, with Dr Carrot skidding along in the rear.

A faint cry of 'Bye, darlings, send my love to Minnie,' wafted towards them on the warm breeze.

Fidge turned round again, and shouted with shock.

Above her, standing in the bus doorway, was Auntie Ruth.

# THIRTY-FOUR

'**G**raham!!!' screamed Auntie Ruth.

A light snapped on, and Fidge saw that her aunt was actually standing in the doorway at the top of the basement stairs in Graham's house, looking down at the two of them with an expression of disbelief.

'We're back!' said Fidge.

She climbed the stairs, Wed Wabbit still tucked under her arm. Graham followed more slowly.

'Hello Mum,' he said, as he reached the top.

'You went down into the basement,' she said, her voice trembling with amazement.

'Yes.'

'In the dark.'

'Yes.'

'In a storm.'

'Yes. Oh, hang on—' Something had caught his eye: the pop-up *Land of Wimbley Woo* book was still lying at the bottom of the steps, and he hurried back down to pick it up.

'Thanks,' said Fidge as he returned.

His mother looked from one of them to the other. 'And you're both filthy,' she said, faintly.

'Yes, it's quite dusty down there,' said Fidge. 'Please could I go and see my sister at the hospital now? I mean, straight away?'

'And I'll come too,' said Graham. 'Could we bring something to eat in the car?'

'Of *course*. What would you like?'

'Anything really. Toast?'

Graham's mother went pink, and tears sprang into her eyes. 'Oh, *Graham*,' she said, proudly, and then hurried out of the room, pausing only to dial a number on her mobile. 'Simon, you'll never believe it,' they heard her say. 'Graham's been down some *steps* and he's going to try some *toast*!'

Fidge nudged her cousin. 'Good thing she couldn't see you dangling upside down from a tree,' she said.

Outside, the storm had broken, and rain was coming down in sheets. Auntie Ruth moved the car so it was right beside their front door, so that Graham could get in without being touched by a single molecule of water, but at the hospital, they had to park a long way from the entrance and despite sharing an umbrella, they were all fairly damp by the time they got inside.

234

'She's on the eighth floor,' said Fidge, brushing the raindrops off Wed Wabbit as they entered the lift.

'I wonder if I can buy a towel in the hospital shop,' said Auntie Ruth. 'And you probably ought to have a hot chocolate to warm you up, Graham. And maybe some throat pastilles just in case. And we should get some antiseptic wipes.'

'I think I'm all right,' said Graham. He was moving his weight from one foot to the other, entertained by the squelching sound his shoes were making. He kept thinking about the pond at the bottom of his garden; he kept wondering what it would feel like to wade right across it.

'And there's a strange little mark on the back of your neck,' continued his mother. 'It looks like green paint. Where did that come from?'

Fidge peered at it. 'Your mum's right,' she said. 'I think you must have got splashed during the explosion. *Green for Daring*,' she added in a whisper.

The lift eased to a stop, the door opened and directly ahead, waiting outside the children's ward, was Fidge's mother.

'Hey!' Said her mum, astonished, as Fidge shot out of the lift and hugged her fiercely. 'That's the best greeting *ever* – I've missed you so much.'

'Is Minnie going to be all right?' Asked Fidge, her face buried in her mother's jumper.

'Yes, really all right. She's asleep again, but we can tiptoe in and put Wed Wabbit into the bed with her.'

'And take this too,' said Graham, holding out the pop-up

book. 'Though it might have got a bit wet.' He opened it to check, and a limp ring of dancing Wimblies flopped out.

'Oh that's a shame,' said Fidge's mother. 'The colours have all run together. You can't tell whether those are supposed to be Yellows or Blues or Pinks.'

Fidge and Graham looked at each other.

'Honestly,' said Fidge, 'I think it's an improvement.'

Minnie stirred slightly as Wed Wabbit was slipped into the bed beside her. Without opening her eyes, she reached out and contentedly curled her fingers around one of his ears.

Mum smiled at Fidge. 'It doesn't take much to make her happy, does it?' she whispered. 'Thanks for bringing him in.'

'No problem,' said Fidge.

# SIX MONTHS LATER

It had snowed on and off for three days, but now the sky was a clear, frozen blue. Graham stood by the open back door. Fidge, who'd come to visit his house with her mum and Minnie, was waiting for him just outside, her breath fogging the air.

'Now are you wearing your fleecy boot liners?' asked Graham's mother.

'Yes,' said Graham.

'And handwarmers in your mittens?'

'Yes.'

'And did you put on *both* thermal vests?'

'Yes.'

'And do you have the special nose warmer?'

'No, because it makes me look like an idiot.'

'And you'll come back in if you're the tiniest, *tiniest* bit cold?'

'Mum, I'm only going out to the back garden.'

She smiled, radiantly. 'I know,' she said. 'And it's *marvellous!*'

Outside, the sunlit snow glittered like a sheet of Christmas wrapping paper.

'Perfect weather for snowman construction,' said Fidge, starting to roll a snowball along the ground.

'I've been researching the best way of doing that,' said Graham. 'It's actually ergonomically superior to make a cylinder rather than a ball.'

'You *know* I've got no idea what "ergonomically" means.'

'More efficient,' said Graham.

'Well let's do an experiment,' said Fidge. 'I'll do my snowball and you do your snow cylinder and in five minutes we'll compare them, and we'll make the one that's biggest into a snowman.'

The cylinder won. It looked like an enormous barrel, lying on its side.

'Impressive,' said Fidge.

'It wasn't my idea,' said Graham, modestly. 'I read about it on a snow sculpture website.'

'It reminds me of something,' said Fidge.

They exchanged a look, and then wordlessly hauled the barrel upright. Fidge smoothed the top of the cylinder so it was flat, and Graham took the round handwarmers out of his mittens and stuck them onto the front of it. Two sticks formed the arms, and Fidge carefully scooped out a long, letterbox mouth.

'It's a Wimbley Wooooooo!' shouted Minnie, rounding the corner from the house. She was dressed from head to foot in a rainbow-striped snowsuit, and was pulling a sledge, laden with toys.

'We could build a whole load of them,' said Fidge. 'And – how about this for another experiment – we could build one on the frozen pond, and then when the ice thaws it should drop straight into the water. Might look quite funny. It's only about a foot deep, so we'll be OK if the ice breaks when we're making it.'

'Good idea,' said Graham, feeling incredibly brave. 'And once it's built I could take a photo of it every few hours as it melts and then put them all together to make an animated film. We're doing that at school.'

'Is it going all right?' asked Fidge. 'Your school, I mean.'

Graham shrugged. 'It's OK. Sometimes it's good, sometimes it's boring.'

Fidge nodded. 'Yup, that's what school's like,' she said.

Minnie took an armful of toys from the sledge. For Christmas she had received three fluffy Wimbley Woos – a Pink, a Yellow and an Orange – and they were her new favourite toys; she placed them side by side on top of the snow Wimbley.

'Where's Wed Wabbit?' asked Graham.

'It wasn't his turn to come,' said Minnie. 'He's got to stay at home and tidy the bedroom. And anyway, you don't say it like that,' she added, loftily, 'because you spell it with an "r". Red Rabbit.'

'Oh right,' said Graham. He raised an eyebrow at Fidge.

She grinned. 'Things change,' she said.

He nodded and grinned back.

Together, they crunched through the snow towards the pond.


Minnie's fifth birthday was a month later.

'It's a book,' she said, inspecting the wrapped present from Grandma.

'Open it, then,' said Mum. 'I think you'll be pleased.'

Minnie tore off the paper, and let out a shriek.

'Wimbley Wooooooooooooooos! A *new* one.' She studied the front cover and picked out the words she could read: '*A . . . of . . . in Wimbley Land.*'

'*A Festival of Theatre in Wimbley Land,*' read Fidge.

Minnie flicked through a couple of pages and then tossed the book to Fidge. 'Read it to me, please.'

'Just a moment,' said Mum. 'Unwrap some of the others first and I'll get you your birthday breakfast.' She caught Fidge's eye and beckoned her into the kitchen.

'Grandma told me that it's not very good,' she whispered.

'What isn't?' asked Fidge.

'The new book. Apparently the rhymes are dreadful, and the colours are all mixed up and they've introduced new characters – an elephant and a . . . a vegetable of some kind.' Her mother's mouth twitched. 'But she thinks Minnie will still love it. So I just wanted to say, you know, try not to be too critical

242

when you're reading it to her. Fidge, you're *already* grinning.'

'I'm not,' said Fidge, grinning.

'Stop it!' Said her mum, fighting back laughter.

'What are you two giggling about?' shouted Minnie.

'NOTHING!' They said simultaneously.

'Hurry up then!'

'Go on, Fidge,' said her mum, giving her a gentle shove.
'And I'll come in with the cake and we'll all cuddle up on the
bed together.'

It was lemon cake, with pink icing. Fidge took a mouthful,
settled Minnie on her knee, and started to read.

*'In Wimbley Land live Wimbley Woos*
*Who come in many different hues*
*And also here are helpful friends*
*With fine advice that never ends.*

*So all these talents make a team*
*And Wimbley Woos can build their dream*
*By listening to others, taking deep breaths and speaking*
    *from the chest rather than the throat, being polite,*
        *trusting their innermost feelings and celebrating the arts,*
*And caring for each other's farts.'*

'It's "HEARTS"!' shouted Minnie.

# Also available by Lissa Evans:

*Small Change for Stuart,*
published by
Penguin Random House
Children's Books

And the brilliant sequel,
*Big Change for Stuart*